M000042018

Robert Roper

Cuervo Tales

New York 1993

Ticknor & Fields

Library of Congress Cataloging-in-Publication Data
Roper, Robert, date.
Cuervo tales / Robert Roper.
p. cm.
ISBN 0-89919-988-7
1. Men — California — Santa Cruz Mountains — Fiction.
I. Title.
PS3568.069C83 1993
813'.54 — dc20 93-145
CIP

Printed in the United States of America
BP 10 9 8 7 6 5 4 3 2 1

To Summer

"We all regret our youth,
once we have lost it."

Marlene Dietrich

Cuervo Tales

CUERVO, CALIFORNIA, IS A LITTLE TOWN IN THE coastal mountains south of San Francisco, half an hour's drive west from Palo Alto and Redwood City. The drive itself is picturesque and energetic, along a curving mountain road that rises and falls steeply as it approaches and surmounts the crest of the Santa Cruz range.

Old-time residents of the area have long affected a backwoodsy manner, though many work "over the hill" and face computer terminals on a daily basis. In truth, Cuervo's outward aspect has changed little in a hundred years. Many of the houses give evidence of their origins as summer vacation cabins from generations ago. Until recently, a local ordinance required that new construction on previously occupied lots incorporate at least a corner from the old building; thus, contemporary monstrosities with multiple decks and hot tubs rise up from humble cabinesque first floors, like weird gigantic mushrooms growing out of a single speck of honest dirt.

What has saved Cuervo from general development, however, making it practically unique in the San Francisco Bay area, is the very steepness of its approach. No full-bore highway can be built over the Santa Cruz crest, given statutory limitations on degrees of rise per mile. To surmount the crest at an acceptable angle, a modern road would have to begin ramping in the middle of the bay itself.

No highway, therefore no bedroom suburb. This simple truth has been hard for developers to accept. The narrow, cliff-hugging road of the last seventy years can bear not one whit more of traffic — witness the fifteen or so fatalities per year, as tourists, day-trippers, and even the occasional Old Cuervo Hand fail to negotiate this or that vengeful hairpin.

But the story of Cuervo is not one of cabins, narrow roads, and retarded development; nor is it one of redwoods, gurgling streams, and poison oak–choked scrub jungles. The story of an inhabited place must be the story of its inhabiters, we humans tend to agree, and in this regard it may be useful to ask whether the locals, taken as a group, exhibit any common characteristics, anything that might be said to distinguish them. One commentator, after many years of haphazard study, feels inclined to answer no, followed by yes. No, because there are many other such communities, self-conscious encampments defined by an isolating geography, scattered throughout California and the West generally. The first fact about such places is always the resentful pride they take in themselves. Nonresidents, or people of short local tenure, are considered beneath notice. Cuervo is truly remarkable in this regard. Inhabitants of twenty years' duration look down on those of only ten; of five years, on those of only three; of three months, on those of only one. To have lived in Cuervo for a long spell is considered a mark of selection rather than, as some might argue, proof of narrow horizons. Someone raised in the canyon, who can claim to be descended from earlier residents, and who continues to live there in no matter how blighted a fashion, is thought to be so authentic as to approach the godlike.

Cuervo, being a town of only about four hundred, thrives on gossip, as do many small towns. It has a single general store, four bars, three churches, and a volunteer fire department that serves as political nexus, where disputes and cliquish feuds often play themselves out.

How, then, is this town distinct — what sets its denizens off, and has for generations? In the first place, there is a remarkable meanness, a sheer willingness to act stupidly toward one another, not to be encountered in towns of the common run. This can hardly be explained without reference to something special, to the idea, perhaps, of some sort of local curse. Area historians (themselves always with axes to grind, grudges to further) generally agree that the canyon was once home to a tribe of the Costanoan Indians, a particularly passive subgroup wiped out, with a gleeful thoroughness, by the first Mexican and American settlers. The Indians, called *corvinas* in the old days (a term of opprobrium whose literal meaning has now been lost), were benign, trusting, and innocently sexual, much like the wild canyon itself, which, when viewed from the high ridges, presents a relaxing vista of rounded haunch-hills, penetrant redwood vectors, and jungly declivities. The first fortunes in the canyon were won by bounty hunters, employees of the local land development company, who earned Mexican silver dollars for every matched pair of Indian lips or ears turned in. (Lipenear Creek, a pretty rill running through redwood glades, eponymously recalls this first industry.) To this day, boys and girls born to "old canyon stock" often exhibit bold features, such as coarse black hair and opaque eyes, that set them off from their fair-skinned, ostensibly Scots-Irish parents, which perhaps should remind us of some two-hundred-year-old rape.

Cuervo has always been a place to escape to — a rough sort of refuge. Mexican highwaymen established the first settlement, in 1804, then fought a three-day battle against troops sent by the Spanish *intendante* (the Battle of Four Vultures, outcome unknown). Deserters from the provincial army, fugitives, cutthroats, cutpurses, trappers, wanderers, and miscellaneous misfits constituted the male population before about 1849, when the American victory over Mexico and the discovery of California gold brought in a new class of person, though probably not a better one. One of the few local industries to do well, in all periods except the modern, was the distilling of whisky. Though not often mentioned in the chronicles of early California history, Cuervo was famous for the cheapness of its liquor and the drunkenness of its inhabitants, and those few archival references to the place (variously known as Corvinatown, Lipenear Canyon, Dingeville, Plummerton, and Crow Canyon before 1910, when it incorporated) all have a tone of frank distaste.

Into this forgotten pocket, onto this blood-soaked, alcohol-stained bit of mountain real estate, came a new type of refugee after about 1950. The Cuervo road, first paved in '53, led cultural rebels more easily up into the hills, away from the stodgy self-celebrations of Palo Alto in the Eisenhower era. Failed Stanford students, untenurable professors, "poets," "musicians," and bohemian types generally came seeking low rents and fresh air, and the town that had never before had a library, a barber shop, a clothing store, a restaurant, or a licensed doctor soon had two coffeehouses, one of them the dingy Cafe Quoi. No one knows what the local inhabitants thought about the sudden influx. Their responses went unrecorded. A middling-famous East Coast poet, disciple of a more well-known Manhattan howler, wrote his "Ecstatic Raga 237" on a barreltop table at the Quoi, according to legend:

> *full moon fifth month in the*
> *penis tree*
> sempiverens *the redwood*
> *in the dead canal*
> *I ate the teeth of starving*
> *dog-eyed children raving blood-*
> *sucking at the star-hole sky*
> *O you priestly savages*
> *this is for Larry Bright-Eyes*
> *suck me in the*
> *mauve dawn O Larry*

By 1962, when the coffeehouses went under, the cultural presence had become less beat, more biker. But now a new influence made itself felt, as veterans of some famous experiments at a nearby psych hospital, where LSD-25 had come rashly into play, retreated to the hills to think things over. This second wave of hip refugees presaged the wholesale invasion of the late '60s–early '70s, when poor, backwoodsy Cuervo became a virtual carnival of communes, countercultural attitudinizing, and starry-eyed drug use. Now raving loonies were sometimes to be encountered on the single downtown street. In the past, anyone wandering half-clothed and red-eyed at noon was likely the victim of alcohol overindulgence; but these new seekers talked of peace and karma and astral projection, some even claiming to have encountered the ghosts of slaughtered *corvina* warriors in the redwood groves. It is from this period, not before, that the local cult of ancient pedigree dates, many of the original families having decided that the Christian-American values they embodied were under threat. Young people either grew their hair long, smoked pot, and sought questionable illuminations, or else they rode around town dressed like cowboys, looking for braless hippie girls to scare. Somehow, this cultural ferment was good for the town, in a commercial sense at least, and several new businesses opened, among them a health food store, an hourly rate motel, and a restaurant called Molloy's.

❧

Cuervo now looks much as the old-timers say it always did — that is, not very good. There is something unconvincing about it. The downtown looks like the set for a TV Western. The houses are all either dilapidated or overweening. The redwoods, the simplest, most primitive of trees, single-trunked and blankly phallic, soar above everything, and the sky above the trees in its two characteristic moods — overcast, baldly blue — induces in most a grumpy sort of lassitude.

Yet people like to live in Cuervo. They come back, after wandering the wide world, some having touched down in really interesting places. There is room in Cuervo to be, to let down your hair. Expectations are low. More than in many American places, people shut their eyes to what their neighbors do. To call this "tolerance" would be to propagandize, yet the net effect is perhaps similar. All during the late '70s and early '80s, for example, young professionals bought crumby cabins, fixed them up, then staged cocaine self-immolations in the woods. Nobody complained.

A rigorous local history, beginning in the eighteenth century and continuing to the present, might descry in Cuervo's past a pattern of successive drug enthusiasms, beginning with alcohol and proceeding through the more modern explorations. Even the *corvinas* (now considered possibly mythic, since no one can point to a living descendant, nor have any artifacts of their culture survived) probably used a local fungus, *parmentis Sissonia,* to induce colorful visions, usually of a sexual or violent nature. Maybe the escape from reality is all that Cuervo has ever been about.

Sometimes, after a lost weekend lasting many years, residents do drift away, to embrace sobriety and a more conventional way of being. One such individual, a veteran of the madcap back-to-the-land days, who figures in the stories that follow, recently returned to the canyon with his teenage daughter, a child who spent her first four and a half years in a spooky cabin in the Cuervo forest. They climbed the long, unpaved driveway to their old house holding hands.

"Oh, Dad," said the girl when they reached the top. "It's not there."

Indeed, their house was gone. Not a stick of it remained. All they could find was a piece from a catenary arch kiln, a device in which the man's ex-wife, the girl's mother, had once fired stoneware pots.

The daughter burst into tears. The man wandered through the weeds of the small clearing where his house once complacently stood, mumbling to himself and pulling his right ear. He saw that there had been a conflagration. Either the fire had been so hot as to leave no debris, or else all the wreckage had been hauled away.

"Don't cry, sweetie," he said distractedly. "It was an old house. It was made of dry wood. It just caught fire, that's all."

But his daughter was inconsolable. She had hoped to visit the site of her earliest memories. She demanded that they leave.

Later, the man returned to the clearing by himself. He was still in shock. Yet he found the place almost beautiful. A bed of rosebushes had grown into a wild thicket. The brush was waist high where his bedroom once stood, where his kitchen had been, where he'd sat on the toilet a few thousand mornings. In this place he and others had led a raucous, heedless existence, having many fine and curious times. His favorite tree, a red-trunked madrone, had been scorched where it faced the house but not destroyed.

He found a fork, the head of a hammer, and the handle from a china cup. But that was all. Despite a prolonged search, he could turn up nothing else.

"Well, trees," he said, "I guess you win. I guess you outlasted us. I know we used to live here, because I remember bits and pieces of it. But there isn't any sign. We've been wiped out."

The trees, second-growth redwoods and tanbarks, maintained a green silence. The man had the impression that they were looking over his head, as monumental adults will sometimes overlook a noisome child.

He continued to poke through the underbrush. It seemed to him that he was about to make a discovery — that some treasure would soon be his.

June 1980

AN ACRE HAD BEEN CLEARED IN THE JUNGLE OF scrub. The earth had baked and become adobe, and here the man and woman laid out their picnic, under a single oak that for some reason had been spared.

"They'll come. It's only two o'clock."

The woman who spoke these words, who was dressed in a beige linen suit, hooked hanks of heavy blond hair over either ear. She busied herself laying out the quiches, the salads. The man had never doubted that they, the other couple, would come. But now he did begin to doubt.

"It's already two o'clock?" he asked.

Below their position, which was on a wild ridge top, an undeveloped canyon ran from right to left. Beyond that canyon was another ridge, likewise covered entirely with scrub, and beyond that ridge were more wild canyons running on to the California coast.

The woman, whose name was Dara Spotts, sold real estate in the area. She had recently purchased this ridge in partnership with several other investors. The acre, which had been denuded and partly leveled by a contractor, was a homesite, one of twelve projected for the ridge.

"Well, if they don't come soon, we can walk down and look at the other sites. Would that be okay?"

"Sure," said the man, who was named Abel Richards.

He was of medium size, thirty-three years old. For today's picnic he had dressed in white slacks and a Hawaiian shirt, the top two buttons left undone. He wore a short beard and canvas shoes.

His eyes were round and bright, tree-green in color. But perhaps his most notable feature was his dense, glossy black hair, thickly curling like the fleece of an unsheared merino.

By tacit agreement, they didn't begin on the food just yet. But the bottle of white wine was warming up, so Richards uncorked it. Dara had brought real glasses wrapped in checkered napkins. They clinked before drinking.

"Here's to you," he said.

"To us," she corrected gently.

Richards had a premonition of embarrassment: not for himself, but for Dara, because her friends, the other couple, might not show. He knew them only slightly. They were to be introduced to him formally this afternoon. Richards had realized only as they were driving up, in Dara's steel-gray Alfa, that the real purpose of this picnic was his presentation as her new guy. He had been uncommonly quiet ever since.

Now, though, the wine acted as a tonic, and he began to see possibilities in the afternoon. One could have worse prospects than the eating of flavorful foods outdoors, on a sunny summer day, in the company of a pretty blonde. Dara had cooked for him twice before. Everything had been so good on both occasions that Richards, who wasn't used to being catered to these days, had been almost tongue-tied with gratitude. That someone would bother to invite him over, then slave in front of a hot stove solely for his enjoyment, bordered on the marvelous, the inconceivable. And yet now, only six or seven weeks after their first evenings together, he was a little uneasy, he was even a little bored with her.

About a month and a half before, gone half-mad with loneliness, he had driven into the tiny town of Cuervo, California, on a Friday night, with the sole intention of meeting someone. His dilapidated mountain home, located two miles outside the town, had begun to seem like a bizarre stage set, where he paced for hours on end in front of an invisible audience. Like this silent, malevolent audience of absent onlookers, he was acutely aware of the odd expressions that sometimes crossed his face as, in the course of conversations he held with himself, he found the words that often eluded him in realer life.

Recently single, he had stopped counting the weekends, the months, without contact of any sort with an adult female. But on this particular Friday his need had been so strong that events, as sometimes happens, took exactly the shape he desired, and he encountered Dara Spotts. This was at the one restaurant in Cuervo that served dinner. Dara was sitting all alone, dressed as if for a date. As soon as he entered she looked him over frankly. Emboldened, he sat at the table next to hers but one. By the time her dessert was being served, they were chatting across the intervening table; by the time his own coffee had arrived, they were seated side by side.

Thereafter, everything went according to schedule: saying that she loved to dance, Dara proposed walking down to Brauch's Tavern, a quarter mile along the Cuervo road, where a local band was going to play. Here they danced for three hours. Dara told Richards the story of her impending divorce. Terry, her second husband, was a hopeless alcoholic, and after years of putting up with his mischief she had suddenly lost all energy for it. The property settlement was going to be a mess, as they were involved in several ongoing deals. Richards was oddly touched by this unsolicited confession; soon to be an ex-husband himself, he appreciated Dara's calm, nonpunitive tone, her refusal to assassinate her husband's character in all the usual ways (aside from labeling him a hopeless drunk). Nor did Dara seem to expect Richards to reciprocate with a frank confession of his own.

He might keep his tale of marital woes, if he had one, to himself. But what he perhaps appreciated most of all was just her acceptance of him, her tacit estimation of him as an all-right guy. This was the first credible sign in a long while that he still belonged to the human family, and Richards felt profoundly, even foolishly, grateful to her.

Only at her house did he begin to feel uneasy. Drinking a cup of peppermint tea, he decided on a course of action which would indicate a certain demure, gentlemanly interest, a desire not to rush things, admirable self-control. Something odd must have been going through her mind, too, because she stopped talking, could hardly look him in the eye anymore. Richards took this for eagerness to have him gone, but at the front door she said:

"Ted's not here tonight. Ted — my little boy."

"Your boy?"

"Well — my teenager, actually. He's sleeping over at the Arnesons' tonight. At his friend Billy's."

Richards understood what this meant. Even so, he thought he ought to go — just leave her in peace for the night. Dara began to look worried, and somehow they fell into a loose embrace. She made a sound against his chest.

"I've been wanting to do this all night," she mumbled.

"You have?"

They went straight from her front door, down a dark hallway, to her bedroom, at the back of the house.

⁂

Seven weeks later, surrounded by untouched picnic foods, they gazed placidly out over the forest.

"Well, it's a good view," Richards observed, "a very fine view. Do the other sites have good views, too? Do they all face this way, what is it, southwest?"

"No. Just this one, unfortunately. But each has a special something. My favorite's down thataway, on the other side of the ridge. It's in a natural sort of bowl. That's where I'd build a house if I was going to live up here."

"Are you going to? Is one of these supposed to be your dream house?"

"No!" she exclaimed positively. "I could never afford it."

Then she proceeded to describe to him, and not for the first time, either, the packaging strategy she had used to gain access to this property in the first place. It had something to do with a friend who sat on the Coastal Commission, who had cleared the way for an unusual division of the acreage. This, in turn, encouraged the bank to make a large loan at a crucial point in time. Richards listened closely, feeling that it never hurt to learn something, that this attractive woman, in her offhand way, knew more about mortgages, perc tests, partnership law, renewable options, and so on than he ever would, even though he, as a man, was supposed to have an affinity for this kind of real-world information. Yet Dara's packaging strategy failed to register, did not penetrate beyond the level of mere logical comprehension. If quizzed on her method in half an hour, Richards would have drawn a complete blank.

By two-thirty, the bottle of wine now entirely gone, he was feeling pretty good. Leaving Dara under the tree he rambled to the edge of the clearing, where a bulldozer, with a hardened wave of mud and scrub still caught in its blade, was massively parked. He climbed on top of the dumb machine, gaining a better view of the forested valley to the west. In ten thousand years, he reckoned, this land had not been altered, never sedentarily settled; since the last Ice Age, which was when the ridges and canyons probably formed, only the occasional naked, acorn-chewing Indian had passed through, with more recently the odd deer hunter or marijuana grower. And now there would be twelve big homes. Richards could summon up no feelings of outrage, not even one of regret; he thought it an interesting idea to take twelve families, of the sort able to afford such housing, and just drop them into this maddening scrub jungle. How would they deal with the poison oak? he wondered. And with the Indian spirits, which, in his tipsy state, could almost be felt and seen, dusty exhalations of the scrub, mysterious vibrations not precisely separable from the smell of crushed bay nuts.

Back at the tree, Dara had moved the food into the shade. With ferocious appetite they now devoured pieces of quiche Lorraine, leafy salad with papaya seed dressing, little French pickles, and cold breasts of chicken. The missing couple was not referred to. Certainly they might have been delayed by a flat tire, but Richards suspected that they'd simply forgotten, had never considered Dara's picnic all that important to begin with. There was something about Dara that made this seem likely. Unhappy with himself for having such an unkind thought, he praised the cold chicken extravagantly.

"It's very simple. You just bake a lemon inside," she explained. "Plus lots of tarragon. Plus a ton of garlic, of course."

"Yes, but it's very good," he replied. "It's the best cold chicken I've ever had, bar none."

"Is it?"

A few minutes later, they left the ridge. Luckily the 'dozer, after grading the top acre, had been driven down over the other side, making a sort of road. The splintered trunks of many small tanbarks lined this route, and the tracks of the machine, incised during the rainy season, had now hardened, which made walking difficult. Dara was wearing alligator pumps with small narrow heels, and after twisting her ankle once she took them off. But her stockings, or rather, pantyhose, would be ruined by the rough going, so she also took them off.

Richards brought along the second bottle of wine. At the third or fourth homesite he placed the bottle in a mossy creek he found, arguing that the running water would cool down the contents somewhat. But this was the very home-site Dara had wanted him to see: the one that was shaped like a bowl. The hillsides rose up gently in all directions, creating an amphitheater effect, a sort of arena of the woods.

"It doesn't get much sun," she commented, "but you could always cut down more trees. Anyhow, I kind of like the shade. It gives a protected feel, don't you think?"

"Yes, it's very beautiful." Richards turned this way and that. "And mysterious — deeply quiet. It's like the woods were waiting for something to happen. Just watching."

"It does have a mystery, doesn't it? Well — think you'd like to live here, darling? Could you get behind that — living up here, in a beautiful new house?"

Richards grinned. "Oh, I could get behind it, all right. But I couldn't afford it. Certainly not if you couldn't."

"But why not? Say I was to build a house up here," she persisted, "a beautiful, special house, just big enough for two certain people. How would that strike you? Would you like that at all — at all?"

Richards' smile became foolish. He blinked several times.

"Think it over," she continued. "Think about it, and when you've thought it through, really thought it through, tell me what you think."

A moment later, Dara sank onto her knees. She took Richards by the hand, pulled him down beside her. They made love there, on the hard forest floor. The wooded hillsides became even more watchful.

Richards kept thinking of the roughness of the earth. Not for a minute could he stop picturing where they were, in a sort of bowl, an open arena of the hills. He imagined furry heads, tiers and tiers of them, many staring eyes, an audience straight out of *Bambi,* watching their every move. The backs of his hands got scraped. Dara's buttocks did, too, he imagined. Then afterward, he was almost afraid to move.

"Are you all right?"

She nodded against his chest.

They dressed in silence, then took the rough path up, Dara humming a thoughtful tune. Just for a moment, Richards wondered what she might have meant — what those thoughts of hers might be. Their feet became entangled, and they almost fell on top of each other. Up near the top of the path, they came upon a strange object. It looked like a doughnut, a nylon or rubber doughnut, just sitting there in the crusty dirt. Richards stared at it in perplexity. Moving forward, he finally understood what it was: just Dara's pantyhose, her rolled-up pantyhose, which she had taken off on the way down. He picked them up and put them in his pocket.

At the very top, as they emerged into the cleared acre again, Dara cried out. Ahead of them was the couple she had been expecting, the good friends she wanted Richards to meet. Taking him by the hand, calling out and waving, she pulled him toward the lone tree.

When Richards' wife left him, he thought that he would be able to stay in the old, remote house they had occupied for many years, but after a few days alone there he felt crazier than ever before in his life. He quickly arranged for someone to house-sit, for an indefinite period, and flew to his brother's place, on the island of Maui.

In a spirit of wanting to slough off all that belongs to the past, he told his brother that he'd never return to the Cuervo canyon, that if he was keeping the lease on the house for the time being, it was only to avoid too awful a feeling of being suddenly rootless. He had been in that canyon, in that same old house, for ten years at that point, since the spring of 1970. Ten years perhaps seems like not so long a tenure, but during that period he and his soon-to-be-ex-wife, Jacqueline, had gone through many notable transformations, from being collegiate, communalist back-to-the-landers, to being a screenwriter and a potter, respectively, a married couple, parents of a baby girl, and so on, and the house had been backdrop to it all. To Richards' surprise, after only four months away he started missing the old place, wondering how it was faring, and since he was desperate to see his daughter anyway he flew back.

The house was not faring well. The couple who had been house-sitting, an unemployed carpenter and his alcoholic girlfriend, had not kept up with the cleaning, and what was perhaps more upsetting, they had moved all their furniture in without taking any of Richards' out, which suggested an expectation of being asked to stay. In its communalist period, the house had been home to as many as twelve people at a time, and only by a harrowing process had Richards and his wife gotten the cast down to manageable size. Really, his best times in the old place — Jackie's, too — had been when they were finally living alone, Richards working on his script assignments, Jackie out in the back yard, making her sturdy pottery in the studio he'd built for her. Those days, or the memory of them, still exerted a powerful influence. So despite what he'd told his brother — that he could never live in the canyon again, that the solitude, now that he needed to meet new people, would be bad, depressing — he toyed with the idea of staying on, seeing if he couldn't make it there for a while.

The house sat at the end of a steep driveway. It was not so far up from the county road, but the drive, unpaved and badly humped, was traversible only by those who knew the trick of it, and this gave the place an impregnable feeling, an air of formidable seclusion. A vast forest began right behind the house, a considerable semiwilderness.

Richards, looking out from his front porch of an evening, could see nothing nearby to suggest the existence of other humans, only a lot of redwoods, a blue-black sky, and a grassy ridge across the canyon. Now and then a car passed on the Cuervo road. The little town itself, of some four hundred souls, was only two miles to the southwest, but Richards had never much liked the place — its cowboy bars, rustic churches, and single country store had never really attracted him, and he knew only three or four people in town.

It was strange to reoccupy his old bedroom. It had been Jackie's and his for so long, and in his absence the carpenter and his girlfriend had slept in it; although the sheets had been changed upon his return, a foreign feeling was palpable, a faint odor and impression of other people. This defeated his attempt to connect to the old feeling, to the sense of this bed's having been the throne, as it were, of his failed marriage. Richards had Margaret, his eighteen-month-old daughter, sleep with him that first night.

The next morning, over a breakfast that he shared with Denny, the house-sitting girlfriend, he explained that he would be staying on alone. Although the place seemed large, what with two bedrooms downstairs, another in the attic, and the studio out back, this wasn't really the case; it was just an old, frail summer cottage, held together with baling wire and plaster, mostly. Furthermore, painful experience over a period of years had proved his unsuitability to group living. In the end, he joked, he hadn't even been able to live with a wife. Denny, who had perhaps been asked to leave other places in her time, merely nodded assent.

That night, he made a dinner for Margaret. She was

"too big" for her high chair now, and not to insult her he set her up on a kitchen chair, using two phone books. Richards had assumed that Jackie, who had moved out some months earlier, would have returned to claim Margaret's high chair, the crib, bath toys, and so forth, but she had taken absolutely nothing with her. This curious lapse was subject to various interpretations, to wit: that she wasn't really serious, would soon be coming back to him; that she had never much liked their dinnerware, a wedding gift from Richards' parents; that she was gone for good, and the proof was in her refusal to be encumbered with material belongings, especially anything reminiscent of their life together. Richards, who was pretty sure now that his marriage was over, was glad about the housewares from a practical point of view, but even so he toyed with the idea of giving it all away or, on second thought, taking his plates ceremoniously out onto his front porch and flinging them one by one down into the canyon. He wouldn't do that, though, and not just because he wasn't a wasteful sort of person; no, it intrigued him, even as it depressed him, to sense his dishes taking on new meaning, to feel them modulating along a symbolic continuum from a position of low-intensity, monochrome denotation ("boring, happily married life") to one more highly charged, more complex ("that former life which, now that it's over, you remember both bitterly and fondly"). This same process of meaning modulation, he noticed, had been going on all over the house, and it was this that had nearly driven him crazy a few months before, when Jackie first left, the feeling that all the trusted symbols of his domestic contentment, his padded rocking chair, his platform bed, his overstuffed sofa, that they'd bought together at a flea market, had begun to mean the opposite of what they should. But this process was now more controlled, more benign. He was only a little afraid that tonight, when Margaret was finally tucked away and he had to face the living room alone, the rank desolation of those first few days would return.

He gave Margaret her bath. She had grown measurably taller, though not less chubby, in his four months away, and her chatter as they played rubber-ducky games was more fluent. After the bath, the brushing of teeth; diapering; they repaired to her bedroom, in the rear of the house, and without any prompting she led him from station to station of the go-to-bed ritual, from changing table to bookshelf, to doll cabinet, to crib. Richards sat down suddenly on a Lego canister, his head in his hands. Margaret, clutching her favorite blanket, watched him quietly from behind the bars of her crib. Finally he stood up, rearranged her pillows and sheets, and stepping into the doorway, he sang "Tender Shepherd" many times in a row, just as he'd done on numerous other nights.

The little girl asleep, he hurried out to the living room. But everything was as he'd left it, and he felt reassured. The house-sitters had pillaged his liquor cabinet remorselessly, leaving only a half inch in a half-pint bottle of crème de menthe. But at the back of the hall closet was a dusty fifth of Heaven Hill bourbon, still about half full. Pouring himself a glass, setting the bottle carefully at his feet, Richards sat back in his rocking chair.

❧

He hadn't meant to stay here so long; remembering the early days, when friends used to bed down all over, in sleeping bags and in hammocks hung from the ceiling, he marveled at the transformation that he'd wrought, the creation of a fairly normal-looking living space out of an old, leaky-roofed wreck. In the early years bats used to squeak in the attic on hot summer nights, sometimes venturing into the lower rooms; Richards, curiously afraid of these harmless beasts, would cower under the sheets while Jackie chased them down with a fishing net. Jackie was the very soul of the house in those days, the warm-eyed, all-welcoming earth mother (or earth daughter, she was so young); most of the energy for repair and alteration had come from her, and they had painted, plastered, rebuilt, and reglazed with a vengeance. A typical case of playing house, Richards now saw — just what one did in one's twenties.

But with Jackie, there had always been a kettle of soup on the boil — figurative bread in the ovens. Richards had believed for years that it was he, with his "cutting edge" personality, who attracted all their many visitors, whereas in fact it was more a case of Jackie's simple warmth, her openhearted way with every kind of troubled soul. From across the wide country they had trekked to his hideaway, an astonishing sampling of the pilgrims of those years: political fugitives, with federal warrants out; macrobiotic fasters; summa cum laude dope peddlers, with bags of cash; psychedelic investigators, some with pretensions to guruhood; painters, musicians, writers, relatives and friends. Jackie had found a way to include them all, to welcome them all. Under her aegis the house had seemed an inviting place, an intriguing sanctuary.

Except that it wasn't really welcoming, not in its heart; the house remained an overbuilt cabin, a rude shack, a wreck with a derelict soul. Only by a series of miracles had it kept from burning down in the years when they heated with a wood stove, and now that there was a gas-fueled central furnace, and the attic had been batproofed and the front windows reglazed, the effect was strangely disorienting, exterior like some abandoned Appalachian hovel, interior like a cozy spinster's cottage in the Berkshires. Uninvited visitors, after slogging up the driveway and catching sight of the house in its nest of tremendous trees, often expressed astonishment, first at anyone's actually living up here anymore, second at the relative modernity of the interior appointments. Instead of finished walls, woven rugs, reading lamps, and a TV, they expected to find a bare puncheon floor, with an idiot child torturing a mouse on a string. Often it was hard to get such visitors to leave, so charmed were they by the house's surprise, its cozy "secret."

The real nature of the place wasn't cozy, though, wasn't genial; one could be fairly comfortable there, warm and dry in winter, cool in summer, but this physical repose was but for the purpose of contemplating one's metaphysical peril (Richards had always secretly believed), for feeling solitary down in one's very bones. The house, which stood on nothing more substantial than a few four by fours, which were sunk in dirt, not cement, which had resisted being uprooted only by another series of miracles, was provisional in the extreme, an unaccountable island of warmth, light, and relative safety in a sea of forested dark. Which was just how one felt — or at any rate, how Richards, now well into the bourbon, was beginning to feel — about oneself, about that part of one's personality that connected to other people, that it was but the frailest, most artificial kind of transitory construction. Just as this old, jerry-rigged cabin sat up here on its spindly stilts, enjoying its illusion of significance, of permanence, he indulged the laughable notion that he was somehow a social creature. The reality was the forest surrounding: the realm of shadow and cold, of furtive beings intent on solitary business. This was his reality, as well, the forgotten "half" of his personality that was by far the more important.

This was why he had stayed on so long; why he'd presided, unconsciously at first, over a steady whittling down of the household, old friends eased out always for this or that good reason, but really just because he hated having anyone else around. When he did the complex accounting in his soul that told him whether it was worth it, whether what he got for making way for someone else was justified, he always came up with the same result. And he had done this with Jackie, too. Never mind the complex rationalizings about "different world views," "changing needs," and so forth, the fact was that he'd acted in a way to drive her off. And now he found himself alone. He had made a little retreat for himself, a Walden Pond without the water, a hermit's nest wherein to sit and stew. Ten years of his life he'd spent in this place, making busy with one thing and another, and only now did his essential purpose show itself clearly; that condition of heart and mind at which he'd been aiming all along.

Sometime during the night, while Richards dozed in his rocker, the empty bottle kicked over at his feet, his daughter called out in her sleep. He awoke and hurried into her room, where he found her tangled up in the blankets. He stroked her forehead. Soon she quieted down; her breathing became sleepish again.

His daughter had asked about him every day of the four

months he was away, according to Jackie; they had a big love going, he knew, and though Richards was sure about nothing else in his life at this point, he was certain that he would never leave her again, not ever. He stumbled back out to the living room.

The house was remarkably silent, he found: a setting moon, just visible through a front window, was spilling pewter-colored illumination out over the dusty rugs. It was a time in the house's night, he felt, when he'd never been awake before, an hour when the hobgoblins came out, or went back in, when a mysterious, portentous alteration in the equilibrium of house forces was getting under way. Richards stood in front of the door to his old bedroom. Listening hard, he could hear nothing but the ominous silence; then he made out something behind it, a subtle, silver-colored sound, the gurgle of the creek that ran through the canyon. Richards had always liked this creek, and he was cheered to hear this sound. As he attended to it, the moment passed, the time of unnerving alteration, and the furniture seemed to exhale all around him. He was cheered by that, too.

Getting into his bed, which he had moved that afternoon to a new position on the floor of his room, he felt that he might still be happy here, living in his old, tumble-down house; he would only have to find some better way.

RICHARDS' YOUNGER BROTHER, JOEL, HAD BEEN living on Maui for almost ten years, and Richards' last impression, formed on a visit lasting four months, was that he was doing well, had most of his wits about him, was unlikely to suffer another of the breakdowns that had so far made his adult life eventful. In 1970 there was an episode brought on by the use of too many psychedelic drugs, a fairly run-of-the-mill, I-am-the-messiah sort of thing, requiring two months' hospitalization. Then in 1974 he suddenly showed up in Berkeley at the home of a mutual friend; penniless, barefoot, but possessed of an unshakable sense of spiritual purpose, he sat in the friend's living room for two weeks straight, saying nothing, eating little, staring intently at the walls. Another spell of sedation and hospitalization brought him around.

Ever since, though — for the last six years — he had been admirably solid. He was a gifted musician, and if most of his income still came not from performing or songwriting, but from selling drugs, this was something that Richards, as the concerned elder brother, had long ago decided that he could "live with," a mere peculiarity of his brother's personality that, in any case, he felt powerless to change.

At the time of Richards' last visit, spring of '79, Joel was living in a cottage near Makawao. He owned two other properties, had countless friends, and for the past six months had been living with a beautiful girl some fifteen years his junior. There was a lot of money around. Visitors came by at all hours, and not just to buy drugs; skillful music was often being made, and the girlfriend, expert in something called "lomi-lomi" massage, led some classes, one of which Richards was encouraged to join. Joel, with his imperturbable manner leavened by trademark flashes of silly wit, presided over his scene agreeably; he had a natural dignity, a philosophical sort of presence, that encouraged in others the desire to sit at his feet. Even the way he conducted his drug business was somehow admirable, Richards felt, not marked by desperation, excessive greed, or trafficking in the more dangerous substances; it was possible to imagine that in another life he might have been a taxes-paying worthy, a stockbroker, say, or a lawyer, someone with a long list of Republican clients.

In early 1980, Richards had a call from the San Francisco airport. His brother announced that he was in town, and he asked to be picked up. Richards drove down from the canyon wondering at the reason for this unseasonal, but not unwelcome, visit. He found his brother in front of the United terminal, barefoot, unshaven, dressed in rags. His only luggage was a battered violin case.

Everything was gone, Joel declared. In a rapidly spoken account that made the previous nine months sound like a spiritual quest, a journey of incomparable significance, he described the loss of his house, his rental properties, his collection of rare acoustic instruments, even his girlfriend — everything had been sacrificed to drug use, he said, to "mystical" experimentation with etherized cocaine. Noelani, the lomi-lomi friend, had gone to live with another man, one better able to fund her own habit. Joel claimed to feel toward her only a "profound love" — he was sure they'd be getting back together.

It was this note, what Richards took for rank delusion on a point of romantic distress, that made him fear for his brother's sanity, since Joel's two previous breakdowns had also, to some extent, been associated with girl troubles. However, in this expectation, at least, Richards was to be disappointed.

Joel moved into the attic room. The cozy upstairs space, once Richards' own bedroom, turned into an appalling shambles overnight, a sort of parody of an addict's den, with sticks of Hawaiian marijuana, a German gram scale, bags of Maneet, the baby laxative, and articles of free-basing paraphernalia spread over all the surfaces. Though penniless, Joel had brought some of his "special substance" with him, and for the first few days he stayed upstairs, venturing down only to use the toilet or to raid the larder, where his taste ran to vast quantities of a single foodstuff (for example, a whole quart jar of organic peanut butter). The two brothers hardly ever spoke. Their schedules were different, and then there was the problem of what to say; should Richards take an inquiring tone, he wondered, or a remonstrating one, or one combining sympathy with non-judgmental dismay ("I'm not saying what you did was wrong, Joel, just stupid, damaging to yourself")? In the end, he took no tack at all, sensing that his brother preferred not to hear from him just yet.

One Wednesday, Richards had to drive to Berkeley to deliver Margaret into his ex-wife's custody. When he returned home he found his brother seated at the kitchen table, with various beakers and burners arrayed in front of him. The mad-eyed adept offered Richards a "taste" from his free-basing pipe, and Richards accepted.

He got high, tremendously high, from but a single puff, and he used the next ten minutes to prove the absurdity of the mind-body problem as conventionally formulated. His brother seemed to understand what he said, indeed, Joel seemed to be sharing Richards' very thoughts, and Richards experienced joyous awe in the contemplation of his own extraordinary mental process. Then the drug wore off. Richards was shocked — deeply, bitterly disappointed. Feeling ill, he stumbled out to the living room to lie down.

His lungs felt seared. His brain was deflated, and now a full-blown depression descended, nor did he fail to note its punishing duration (seven times as long as the high, at least). As Richards promised himself that he would never do this again, never lacerate his soul and system by this evil means again, he heard his brother back in the kitchen, lighting up several more times.

The next day, a summery morning of earth smells, cornflower skies, and vivid new grass on the distant hill-sides, as happens sometimes in a California February, Richards met his brother on the front porch. As they sat in the yard with their shirts off, Richards began to speak, then to rant, about what Joel had done to himself; despite an original intention to go easy, to make some points in a gentle, nonthreatening manner, he got carried away, but Joel, not cowed at all by Richards' brutal accusations, came right back in the same spirit, marshaling arguments for "drug pioneering" with an ingenuity that Richards could hardly match. How his poor, mind-blasted brother, after nine months of daily and nightly pipe sessions, which had reduced him to a mere one hundred thirty pounds, giving him the look, now, of a true madman, could continue to put one word in front of another, let alone make sense, Richards simply didn't understand. The very fact of his eloquence — his easy impersonation of a captious, unprincipled verbal maneuverer, in a style highly typical of their entire family — was somehow significant to Richards, almost moving, and he fought back an urge to declare that, as long as they could go at each other like a couple of rabid lawyers, everything was sure to turn out okay.

The actual effect of their argument, however, was to make relations worse, and Joel retreated to the attic room. From here he sent messages of chill that permeated the whole house. It was during this period, seventy-two hours when Richards saw him not once, heard only an occasional thump through the ceiling floorboards, that his supply of drugs must have given out, and he was driven downstairs by boredom or possibly a return of normal appetite. Always a graceful, athletic figure (he had been a halfback in high school), Joel passed Richards in the hall of the house with an exaggerated, sweeping aplomb, as if about to set off, as soon as he got by this insignificant obstacle, on some magical errand. Despite the cool evenings he dressed as for Hawaii: cotton shorts, bare feet, a polyester tank top. Occasionally he assumed yoga postures on Richards' living room rug. Richards, heading out to the kitchen, there to pour himself yet another cup of strong coffee, to help eke his paltry daily production of sentences, saw his brother twisted up like a fakir, sweat pouring off his back, his ventilations sounding forlorn, angrily forlorn, in the otherwise silent house. Then on other mornings, Joel established himself on the living room sofa, on several pink pillows; with legs demurely crossed, hands folded prayerfully, he remained immobile for hours but for the ritualistic lighting of cigarettes.

After a week and a half of this phase, Richards began to take heart. Though they still weren't talking, his brother had condescended to take a few meals with him; furthermore, it was becoming clear that Joel, though deeply disturbed, seriously unhappy, wasn't really "crazy" this time, not psychotic-breakdown-type crazy, with active delusions and the whole kit of related symptoms. His main emotion seemed to be impatient disgust, a fairly appropriate response, Richards thought, to the situation he found himself in. But the real reason for Richards' optimism was just the end of the mad pipe business. It was now ten days since his brother's last indulgence, nor did he seem to be suffering a painful withdrawal. As if to advertise how controlled he was, how in command of his appetites, he had even stopped smoking marijuana, for the first time in fifteen years (normally he rolled a fat joint while still in bed in the morning, then puffed others throughout the day).

Another week passed. Returning home one rainy afternoon, Richards heard half a conversation going on upstairs, on the phone extension there; he took note of its length — twenty-four minutes — only hoping this wasn't a day-rate call to Maui. Then later that night, as he was falling asleep, he heard two other calls go out, jaunty communications involving much hearty laughter.

He had never considered that his tortured, confused, utterly penniless brother might not be without certain personal resources. He tried to think of friends of Joel's who lived in the area, people he might be contacting for social reasons alone, yet Richards' suspicious mind kept recalling for him his brother's more customary use for the telephone. Three days later, a stranger appeared on the porch, a short man with scuffed shoes and a passing resemblance to the French crooner Charles Aznavour. The stranger asked to speak to Joel.

Ten minutes later, the feckless recluse finally ambled down from the upstairs. He was freshly shaved, dressed in clean clothes — Richards recognized them, with a start, as some of his own — and he exuded a casual bonhomie, a *ça-va-sans-dire* sort of self-assurance. The impression was that of someone busy with important matters who, however, could spare just a moment, who might even condescend to do a favor for an old friend. The stranger talked of days gone by, reminding Joel of an embarrassing encounter in Aspen, Colorado ("That was fucking priceless, man. You really blew her mind"); then he extracted a brick-shaped package from a shopping bag. Joel recalled an even more bizarre little contretemps, something involving a Ford Ranchero and two Filipino women, one thin, the other with huge breasts, and in the meantime he put a pinch of fine, pearlescent powder in a pipette that contained clear liquid. At this point, the stranger glanced dubiously at Richards, who had been watching.

"Oh, he's just my brother."

"I didn't know you had a brother, Joel. Hello there — Joel's brother."

As soon as the stranger was fairly out the front door, Joel hurried back upstairs. Richards could hear the test tubes and beakers being brought back into play. This no doubt signaled the beginning of another weeks-long "pipe session." In the downstairs of the house, Richards roamed furiously from room to room.

He would throw his brother out; just on account of the risk he had been made to run, without so much as a by-your-leave, he felt justified, although the details of so drastic a move, the practical aspects of it, were deeply troubling. Should he throw Joel out forthwith, simply send him packing; or, considering how far away his home was and how broke he was, should Richards lend him money, enough to get there in safety? Or — being more prudent still — should he loan him money *and* buy him a plane ticket, see him pretty much safely on his way back to the islands? The problem with this last option — the most helpful, the most genuinely brotherly — was that it might be construed as weakness on his part, as endorsement of unacceptable behavior; but by the same token, should his brother go to the airport with that kilo in his pocket, then start raving at some ticket counter, the likely consequences were such as Richards preferred not to contemplate.

But he had to take a stand, he felt: had to put his foot down. To allow Joel to stay on at his house, to continue to ruin himself — and who knew what would happen when Charles Aznavour, in a few days' time, learned that his package had not been transported swiftly and safely to Hawaii — would be to acquiesce, not only in criminal behavior, but in a self-destructive course of the sort an older brother was required to oppose. Joel was weak, Richards told himself; obviously, an addict of some kind. Some enduring, fundamental deficiency of character had produced in him the need to consume potent, mind-altering agents on a daily basis, something, anything, that might rescue him from the dread experience of ordinary consciousness. Richards, whose own tendency, as he had gotten older, was in the other direction, actually had a hard time understanding this orientation. Exactly to the extent he felt his life wasn't going so well, was slipping past him, turning out to have been based on false assumptions, he had a desperate need to feel it "as it was," to take it neat, not so much because clear thoughts and right sensations might point a solution as because they seemed at times the only consolation. But Joel was different. Some irregularity in metabolism, some slight pharmacological imbalance, had caused him to choose to live in this dangerous way, to seek oblivion. Yet the real question, the truly troubling issue, on which Richards' determination to act continually foundered, was: How did you turn your back on such a pathetic character? How, knowing full well his "disability," did you then toss him out on his ear? Deny him the sanctuary of a brother's hearth and home — deny him a brother's compassion, when this was all that stood between him and disaster?

Some two hours later, as Richards continued to pace and obsess downstairs, he heard the phone being used again in the attic. Then at dinnertime, the "addict" himself, the poor devil who, in Richards' thinking, had attained by now the status of an utter invalid, came breezily downstairs, packed and dressed for travel. He had called the airport and, as luck would have it, there was a single seat remaining on a

PSA flight at nine-thirty. No problem with payment, Joel declared: he still had his VISA Gold Card. If Richards couldn't drive him over to the airport, he was prepared to hitchhike; if worse came to worst, he could always call a cab.

On the drive over, Richards kept marveling at the transforming power of having a felony to commit. His brother looked more like his "normal" self now than at any time in the previous three weeks, that is, like a calm, basically reasonable individual, a manly sort of fellow with a certain presence. They talked about Richards' daughter and along other noncontroversial lines. At the airport Richards stood by quietly, if nervously, while Joel transacted his business at the ticket counter, then passed a blue daypack, containing the kilo of cocaine among other things, through the security x-ray. Richards had planned to stop right here — just say good-bye, go outside and start to breathe again — but for some reason he followed his brother through the checkpoint. In silence they proceeded down a broad, sparsely peopled corridor; Joel, with his daypack slung casually over one shoulder, a cigarette occupying his other hand, had given Richards his fiddle case to carry.

Soon they became aware of a disturbance up ahead: a murmurous roar, a sound like water surging around the piles of a pier. The corridor forked and they found themselves in a broad lobby, which was jammed now with Hawaiian travelers, prospective vacationers numbering in the hundreds.

Just as they arrived, a flight attendant, dressed like a renter of cabanas on the beach at Waikiki, picked up a mike and made the final announcement to board. In response to which, those travelers not already on their feet, not already formed in a long, snaky line three or four people abreast, arose. The level of hopeful chatter, of sweetly anticipatory human excitement, increased palpably, and Richards, whose response to crowds was generally nervous, self-defensively ironic, instinctively held back. But his brother plunged right in — took up a place at the front of the line, and from this position, with an eager, good-natured expression on his face, surveyed his companions.

Now the line started to move forward quickly. Richards, inching along on a roughly parallel course, two or three feet behind his brother, sought vainly for something comical to say, some reference to sunburns to come, Bermuda shorts, Holiday Inn luaus, and the like.

Joel, beckoning him closer, seemed to want the fiddle case back. But it was Richards himself whom he suddenly clasped, held to his chest with clumsy force. Wordlessly embracing, gasping like a couple of wrestlers, they stumbled together over a short distance full of strangers, and only as the door of the gate approached, the flight attendant holding out a hand for boarding passes, did Richards' brother turn without a word and let him go.

RICHARDS GOT LOST, BRIEFLY, ON THE STREETS leading into the hills of Berkeley, where relaxed houses rambled up and down vertiginous lots, and the cars parked at the curb were all *recherché* foreign: Renaults, Citroëns, the odd Facel. On the seat beside him was a doll, to be given to his two-year-old daughter. Many years before, Richards had been a graduate student at the university in Berkeley, and he had gone to visit a professor one night at home; the professor, an authority on the antebellum South, had lived in an elegant stone and oak-beam house on one of these same winding streets. In the course of that evening Richards realized that he held no future in the academy. That night, which he hadn't thought of in at least ten years, now returned to him with embarrassing clarity: had he really described the head of their department as "a jackass and a poseur," while accusing the history faculty in general of "right-wing tendencies, time-serving, arse-licking, the whole hateful bag of slimy scholarly tricks"?

But here was the street he wanted. He had more or less stumbled upon it. Rather than park in front of the house, where his approach might be observed, he left his car around the corner and walked back, holding Margaret's doll by the heel. The house where his estranged wife was living now was set at an odd angle to the street, and several beds of poorly tended rosebushes made the yard into a sort of maze. A small red wagon, rusted and grown around with weeds, rested near the bottom of the front steps. Richards recognized it suddenly as one of his gifts, another of his well-intentioned, lovingly selected offerings to Margaret: were all of them treated in this way, summarily abandoned, left out in the wind and rain?

No one answered his knocking. But Jackie had promised to be home, so he wouldn't have driven up for nothing. He knocked extra hard, and the door opened with a liquid squeal, as if the house itself were crying out. Harry, Jackie's new boyfriend, peered out at him distrustfully. Harry was a handsome man, fifty-plus, dark of visage; he was dressed this morning in a soiled silk kimono, with rubber flip-flops on his feet.

"I say . . . Didn't think you'd make it, old man. Bit of all right, that. How's the hand, hmm? Can't remember when we saw you last. December? Whitsuntide, was it?"

Richards replied, "Hi there, Harry, old fellow. It was only two weeks ago. You were real drunk, and you threw up on my car bumper. Is Margaret inside? Jackie?"

Harry was a screenwriter; Richards had heard of him, had even met him once, long before Jackie ever took up with him. Previously a "constructivist" painter, a fairly well-known New York figure, he had grown tired of the scene in his mid-thirties; for no particular reason, he had emplaned for Los Angeles, where, within a matter of weeks, he knew almost everybody. Jack was still "pre-" in those days, and they had palled around, committing notorious high-jinks together; the story was that they had shared a few girlfriends, among them, the nervous blonde with the delicious overbite, the one who played with Jack in the piano movie. Harry wrote script after script, none of them ever getting made, but he was earning a comfortable living, what with option payments and so forth. Then after many years, the first really big Jack project, the famous one set in a loony bin, came his way. For six weeks' work cowriting he earned $700,000, plus a half a point of the gross. He had not worked since.

"Jolly good . . . I say. Is that for me? Is that my very own dolly? Lovely, little red dolly . . . Jolly good . . ."

He wasn't British; he came from Baltimore, Richards knew, from the Jewish suburbs. Richards envied the man his success, but having gotten to know him lately Richards felt creepy in his presence, vaguely repulsed. All those years of toil in the Hollywood vineyard, then lightning strikes, and the problem becomes survival of another kind: no need to work anymore, inspiration flown, and hi there, pal, come with me to the bathroom. Let us make us happy. Someone said that he was sick now, that his health was "compromised." Could it be a lymphoma, or was it only the speedballs? A kind of soiled glamour attached to him, a shroudlike covering of semifame. When Richards first heard, not long after his breakup with his wife, that she had taken up with the famous Harry L., gone to live in his house, he experienced something more than the predictable spasm of jealousy. Of all the overfunded, burnt-out wastrels he knew of in L.A., this was the one who truly seemed to live under a black sun, who was indubitably destined for something ugly. That Richards' own daughter would now be spending time in the man's partial custody, traveling back and forth in his cars, his speedboats, and so on, gave Richards even more of a turn.

Once inside, he felt completely lost. The house was almost entirely dark. Harry had disappeared. All the drapes had been drawn against the day, and the air in the front rooms was foul and overused. Half-stumbling through a doorway, Richards came into a parlor full of shin-creasing furniture, where there obtained a strong smell of dog. He remembered now that Harry owned a Great Dane, a scabby, brindled bitch with a broken tail, which Richards had once tried to befriend. As he fumbled for the animal's name, something hit him hard at thigh level, and he cried out in surprise. But fangs did not tear into his flesh, and a moment later, as he groped downward, he felt pudgy arms, small round shoulders, a warm, silken head. "Daddy!" this package squealed in a high, impossibly bell-like voice; "Daddy-Daddy-Dads!"

Richards lifted her up quickly. He held her against his chest, his heart still thumping from the anticipated dog attack. "Margaret? Is that you? Come here, sweetheart," and he kissed her in the vicinity of her right ear.

"Baby," he went on. "Darling. I brought you a present . . . Here, can you feel it? Take it. It's a little doll. She's a lot like Red Doll — like the one you lost."

"Daddy, Mommy says Red Doll's gone to the bad place," his daughter said in the dark. "She says they're gonna use her for stuffing. In somebody's mattress."

"Mommy said that? Really? Well — she had to be kidding. Red Doll's all right. I hear she's gone away on vacation. She's gone to Tahiti, I think . . ."

Surging forward, Richards soon hit a swinging door, which delivered them into a kitchen. Here, in a scene of remarkable disorder, the Great Dane held sway: with whirling feet that didn't grip, that clicked and clacked because her toenails needed clipping, the bony animal arose and rushed at them pell-mell across the linoleum. Richards braced himself for the inevitable impact. But from the safety of his arms, Margaret shouted "Down, Frankie! Get down!" in a tone of unmistakable command no doubt learned from some adult. The dog immediately obeyed.

A moment later, rolling onto her back, she revealed a dirty belly, with four sets of lifeless, wizened teats.

Every inch of kitchen countertop, Richards now noticed, every cubic centimeter of sink space, was occupied with dirty dishes or cooking utensils; the floor of the kitchen itself showed the remains of many other meals, with bowls, skillets, fondue pots, and aluminum steamers piled high under a butcher-block table. Ever the meticulous housekeeper, Richards sniffed around disdainfully for a while, noting that the pans on the floor were cleaner than those in the sink, probably because the dog had been allowed to lick them.

"Come on, Margaret," he said. "Let's get out of here. It doesn't smell so good, does it?"

"Down Frankie — down!" his daughter continued commanding, as Richards carried her out to the back patio.

❧

Thirty minutes later, when his wife still had not appeared, Richards began to feel offended. Margaret was watering some rosebushes along a fence. On the phone the night before Jackie had sounded friendly, almost eager to have him come up and visit; then again, she was erratic these days, amazingly various in her moods, or maybe she was simply sick, or was sleeping in today. The patio was bare but for a chaise longue, a folding chair, and a cast-iron table missing its glass top. The yard beyond was like a desert: not a single weed or blade of grass was still alive, and the ground had begun cracking up into adobe cakes. Margaret looked a lot like her mother, Richards mused as he watched her play in the yard; during the weeks of his custody, he could fool himself into thinking she looked like him, like his side of the family, but in fact she had exactly her mother's vivid, even features, the pouting mouth, eloquent little nose, shiny black-brown hair, bittersweet-chocolate eyes. With a feeling like falling inside of him he noticed now that she wasn't wearing any diapers, just a pair of tiny cotton panties, with a pattern of pink balloons; that this great change, end of the era of incontinence, had occurred on Jackie's watch rather than his own made him morose.

Just at that moment, his soon-to-be-ex-wife came out of the house. Richards heard her sit back on the lounge chair, and after a moment he slewed around, intending to say hello. She was drinking white wine out of a tall glass.

"Like some water? Or what — a beer?"

"I don't think so, Jackie," he said, sounding a little stiff. "It's ten o'clock in the morning."

"That's right. We're out of beer anyhow."

Jackie had lost weight. Never more than slender, she looked positively anorectic now, and Richards was evilly gratified to see this change. The sun annoyed her, and she maneuvered her chair to sit in a shadow cast by the roof.

She apologized for not being up when he arrived. They had had guests the night before, among them, Harry's old Hollywood agent, who was now a Jungian therapist practicing in Berkeley. The agent had gotten drunk and had raked up old financial disagreements.

"If Harry gave away all the pieces that people say they have a right to," she explained with intense, borrowed resentment, "he'd be bare bones. He'd be like that bush over there. Stripped naked."

Richards had loved Jackie, in his way, for many years; but toward her physical self he had always had an odd feeling, something more disinterested, less romantically compelling, than he had imagined he could feel toward a wife. Her boyishly able body and her simple, vivid face, *très gamine,* as people liked to say, had always evoked in him a feeling not quite immediately, or even predominantly, desirous, a feeling more nearly brotherly, with strong components of protectiveness and of sexless admiration. He thought of this now as his response to her appearance deepened, and he felt as he imagined her father might feel, the way he would have felt if, for instance, he had given Margaret to someone for safekeeping and she had been returned to him in an all-over-bruises condition. Not that she showed outward signs of misuse, but her health seemed questionable, undermined somehow; that quality of milky, sweet-natured youth and poise, which had always been hers before, which he had assumed would always be hers, was amazingly gone. She looked ashamed about something: irritated, exhausted. What particularly distressed him was the condition of her hair, once glossy, resinous, and thick, with the prune-Danish smell of a true brunette's; it had been reduced to resemblance to black straw.

"What *is* it with your hand?" she asked, doubtless disturbed by his scrutiny. "You're holding it funny. There — when you do it that way. Just like that."

Richards looked into his lap. His right hand rested between his thighs, the fingers curled under demurely. What was odd, if anything, was simply the way the hand seemed to be burrowing in: as if it wanted to hide inside his own body.

For want of anything better to speak of, Jackie now began to tell him about last night, about the scene when Harry's old agent had come to call. The agent, known now as "Dr. Ariel Chance," was a student at the Jungian Institute in San Francisco, and he had told them a story going the rounds over there.

"One of their senior analysts, someone with a big name, went to Norway last summer, to the World Psychoanalytic Conference . . . just an excuse for a vacation. After the conference, he traveled up north, to Knut Hamsun's ancestral village — you'll like this, Richards, you've got the same proto-fascist taste in literature — and on the way, he met another analyst, also an American, who was also interested in Hamsun. They made their pilgrimage together, and then the other guy suggested that they continue on north, way up to the Arctic Circle, where there's supposed to be great salmon fishing. The guy from San Francisco wasn't much inclined at first, because he doesn't like to fish, but he finally went.

"You know how it is when you meet someone traveling: if there's anything in common, it seems significant somehow, like fate had put you together. Everything shows up a little stronger over there, although, if you met the same person back home, you'd probably avoid him, since it's no fun being around people just like you. They took a ferry or something up the coast, then drove north on dirt roads. After a hard trip they got to the area they wanted, where this big river dumps into the sea. They set up their tent right on the beach, right where a river runs out.

"Then they caught a bunch of fish. Since they couldn't keep them fresh for very long, they split them open, just like the Eskimos do, and dried them in the sun on planks. After a few days their camp was full of drying fish. Then one evening, just as they were going to bed, they heard noises out in the camp. One guy stuck his head out of the tent, to see what was going on, but he couldn't tell. So he went outside to investigate.

"The other guy — the one from San Francisco — waited inside the tent. When his friend didn't come back in ten minutes, he went out to check things himself, and he found everything a mess, the whole camp torn up. It looked like a war, like something had come through there tearing up all the fish. He kept looking for his friend. Then he saw him, down by the water, just flopping around there, kind of slapping around in the waves. The guy from San Francisco yelled to him, then he ran down to him, across the beach. When he got closer he saw his friend was just lying on his belly, like he was about to go out for a swim. The guy from San Francisco went in the water, and he held him by the foot, but then something came up . . . this big thing, a huge shape, rose right out of the water. And it had his friend's head in its mouth. It was a bear — a polar bear. I guess they have them up there, cruising up and down the coast all the time. It kept pulling in the other direction . . . They wrestled over his friend for a while, but the bear was too strong. It just swam out to sea, holding his friend by the head . . ."

Jackie drank off her glass of wine. Richards watched intently — he seemed deeply perplexed. Margaret, who had started to water the bushes again, glanced over at her parents; her mother's tone of voice must have attracted her, or maybe she recognized the name "polar bear."

"It just pulled him out to sea," Jackie continued, "then munched him, I guess. And the other guy realized there was nothing he could do, of course; and that he was all alone, about a hundred miles north of the Arctic Circle. Then he thought that this bear might be coming back — coming for him. So he got out of there fast. And now he's very troubled, he's dropped his practice. I hear he's been consoling the widow, who has four kids. They say he has hideous dreams — archetypal dreams, I imagine, since he's a Jungian . . ."

Margaret dropped her hose, and she said chirpily, "I had a dream too, Mommy. And there was a big bear in it. It was eating people up. It even ate Daddy. It was yucky."

Jackie waited a moment, then asked calmly, "Do you mean that the dream was yucky, Margaret? Or that Daddy was yucky to eat? Which one is it?"

Margaret pooched out her lips, opening her eyes very wide. Then Jackie laughed, and she called her over to give her a hug.

Richards was quiet for a while. He stared out at the yard, where the hose continued to drain into the ground. His right hand had disappeared between his legs.

He was starting to take seriously an urge he had had a few minutes earlier: an impulse just to pick his daughter up, take her away, never let go of her again. These days their agreement stipulated that Margaret was to spend two months with one parent, two with the other; for more than a year they had worked things out, overcoming their disagreements in the interest of acting predictably where the child was concerned, but now Richards felt that all bets were off, too much had been thrown in his face all at once. He didn't like this talk of bears that ate people's heads; just as he hadn't much liked the joke, as Margaret had reported it, of Red Doll being used for mattress stuffing. If Jackie had looked a mess herself but the house had been in fair order; or if the house had looked, felt, and smelled as strange as in fact it did but she had herself seemed in possession of herself; or if she had at least bothered to be fully conscious when he arrived, then he might not have considered taking this drastic step. But now he was in the position of having been shown too much — given too many pretexts. Maybe Jackie herself hoped that he would act: unconsciously wanted him to take this impression, see how things really were with her.

She seemed utterly changed now; a complete inversion of the woman he had always known. The hippie princess, young earth mother, maker of womb- and egg-shaped pottery, planter of organic gardens, was inexplicably gone, completely vanished; to be replaced by this cadaverous figure, this drinker at 10 A.M. She looked like a dweller in New York basements — a figure from a Warhol film, perhaps. Her feeling toward him was not so much bitter as it was incomprehensible, and in her company he became, as now, sadly perplexed, nearly speechless. Yet the important issue, the essential question, was whether she was a fit custodian for Margaret, given her current condition. And on this score, Richards had to admit to even more perplexity. Margaret seemed well fed; her clothes were new and clean (or had been so before he let her play with the hose); her chirpy, spunky spirit was much in evidence, nor did she ever resist being sent back to her mother's house after staying a while with him. He couldn't make himself believe that Jackie would ever neglect their child — all those seasons spent up in the mountains, those years dedicated to "the enduring human values," to earth-goodness, and so forth, had to count for something, didn't they? Now Jackie needed to throw that life over, because it represented the years she had wasted with him; but surely her original impulse had been genuine, said something about who she really was.

She got up suddenly, and when she came back out she had several crayon drawings of Margaret's, each of them such a scrawled, stick-figurish creation as to amount to a brilliant parody of "child's art." Richards looked at them closely, finding that he was just as inclined as Jackie to see signs of an unusual talent.

"Great use of color," he declared. "Sort of fauvist — well, Matisse-like, anyway."

"She's still pretty free with it," Jackie agreed. "But she reminds me of you sometimes. When she makes a mistake, she gets mad and tears the whole thing up. Just hates it — hates it."

"Why is that being like me?"

"Are you *kidding?*"

They had a small laugh together.

Richards proposed a change: a return to an earlier, simpler system of child-shuttling. Instead of two months with each parent, why not two weeks, as they had done at the start? Jackie said that she had preferred that system, too, but now, since she was in L.A. half the time, living at

Harry's other house, it didn't make sense. Poor Margaret would have to get on an airplane every two weeks, which was surely too much. Richards confessed that when he didn't see his daughter for a long time, he went a little crazy; he was in love with the brat, addicted to playing daddy, and who would have ever expected this? Jackie laughed, saying that it was absolutely predictable: all it had taken for him to fall selflessly in love with a female was that she be no more complicated than a three-year-old.

Richards laughed then, somewhat through his teeth.

He left soon after. A peculiar exhaustion overtook him, a feeling of having too many feelings, too many thoughts in his mind at once. At the front door something like a spasm of pure sadness passed through him, an electric current of rue. He had created this mess, he suddenly knew, he was its principal author; the strange condition of this woman, once so healthy and sensible, so outwardly comfortable with herself and the world, and the dilemma of this poor child, who was now to be suspended between the two of them forever, somehow this was all his doing, the creation of his heedless, unaccountable will. He couldn't say by what discrete, unthinking steps he had brought this about, subverted the family they had started out to be, but the responsibility was his. As he mused along these lines, Margaret, who had already kissed him good-bye inside the house, rushed from the dark interior and weakly attached herself to his knees. Richards had to pry her off, and as he did so, Jackie took her by the hand, pulled her back toward the doorway. The girl started to cry then, halfheartedly; and Richards went quickly down the steps.

RICHARDS WALKED FOUR MILES ON FOREST PATHS one day hoping to find a friend, Martin Declan, at home. Martin's house was high up a wooded canyon. There was no phone and, as had happened once or twice before, Richards found the house empty, the front door open and Martin nowhere in sight. Thinking he might return soon, Richards got himself a beer out of the refrigerator and established himself on Martin's front porch, in a broken-down armchair that overlooked the forest.

The house — just a shack, really, much like Richards' own semiderelict cabin — belonged to someone who lived out of state who, finding Martin camped nearby one day, had hired him to look after the property. Martin was always falling into situations like this, houses that needed guarding, great properties that wanted a caretaker, and people in the remote canyon actually competed for his services. He was likable and, in a way, dependable; as a lifelong resident of the canyon, he was thought to afford "credit" to those who associated with him in some way.

After about an hour Richards heard rustlings on a path above the house. A moment later Martin came into view.

He wore dusty work clothes and a small army surplus knapsack. Rather tall, with extremely wide shoulders, he had let his hair grow long over the winter, and this blue-black mane gave him something of the look of an Indian. He sat down lightly beside Richards, making no sign of welcome. He smelled of sweat and new leaves.

"That better not be my last beer."

Richards was by now drinking a second.

"Digging a few holes in the woods, by some chance?"

Martin smiled. A moment later he went in the house.

When he returned, he brought a pound slab of cheese and a rolled-up tortilla, and he took alternate bites of these. Green hot sauce dripped from the unbitten end of the tortilla. When he inclined his head to bite, his hair swung forward and obscured his face.

From the condition of his clothes, it was clear to Richards what he'd been doing in the woods. Richards knew him to have grown marijuana in the past, and in a sense it was unreasonable to expect him not to, what with spring well launched and several hundred wild, wooded acres at his disposal. The owner would never know unless he happened to ask Martin, who would probably not have denied it. The chances of his remote gardens being discovered by hikers or hunters were slim, nor had they ever been seen from the air by county sheriffs in helicopters.

It was late April. Buckeye and lilac trees were still flowering, after a wet winter, and at the edge of the clearing that served as Martin's front yard a true jungle began. It was not the sort of jungle giving an impression of suffocating warmth, of humid fertility, rather it was one whose essence is prickliness, brittleness, scented astringency. This tangled growth would have to survive the sun-blasted, rainless summer and fall of the California midcoast, and for purposes of water retention it was therefore more closely woven than anything in Brazil or Sumatra. It was in its most densely impenetrable sectors, in the monkey-bush and poison oak thickets, where even the deer and wildcats preferred not to go, that Martin put his gardens.

Fifty yards below the house, along the path Richards had followed getting up here, old redwoods grew. They made a completely different sort of world. They had rooted on either side of a wild creek, and looking beyond Martin's front yard, across the canyon formed by the creek, a nearly vertical wall, entirely covered in gray-green scrub, rose to a height of some four hundred feet. Somewhere between the house and that immense wall, along a tributary of the creek, Richards had gone on a bow hunt with Martin once, an expedition not successful in terms of animals killed but memorable, at least for Richards, for its calm, noncompetitive spirit, miles and miles hiked along mysterious game trails, hours spent expectantly, if in the end unprofitably, high up a maple tree over a salt lick. Martin almost always took a buck or two a year, if not with bow then with rifle. Richards, as he gazed at that enormous wall of scrub, now got it in mind to ask about this year's season, to suggest to Martin that they go out together again.

Before he could broach this subject a violent thrashing caught his attention. A tawny dog burst into the clearing.

Richards half-rose to his feet, and his chair skittered back. Martin meanwhile kept to his spot, his legs dangling over the porch edge. The dog rushed up with an alacrity that Richards didn't like, but Martin merely raised his face to it, his hands caught between his knees. The animal began to lick his face, with coy inclinations of a huge, St. Bernard–ish head.

"You bastard," Martin finally said. He pushed the monstrous head away.

Growing less animated, the dog now allowed Richards to look it over. Impressively muscular, like a Lab but much taller, it had coarse, tightly curled, mud-colored fur. On its chest was a patch almost perfectly circular and purely white. The audacious, slavering head, frightening but for a somehow generous expression, came to seem more bulldogish than St. Bernard.

"Is this yours, Martin — this raging monster?"

"No. I don't claim that honor."

"It seems to think it belongs here."

The dark-haired man contemplated the tawny animal. "I don't know whose it is. Probably it just came up from town. Dogs wander up here all the time. Then they get out on the ridges, and they start chasing cows. The ranchers shoot 'em."

"So you think this one's going to get shot?"

"Probably. If it likes to run cows."

Both men bent over the attentive dog now. The beast, subsiding onto a broad flank, sighed deeply, as if in stoic acceptance of its probable fate.

Half an hour later, while Richards used the bathroom in the house, he heard a woman's fluting laughter. Returning to the front porch, he found Martin talking to someone he half-recognized.

He couldn't remember her name, but before he could put his mind to figuring out what she was doing up here, he experienced an odd shock, that peculiar sensation we have when we encounter someone familiar who, however, lacks some crucial element of his normal getup. Richards looked her over as if expecting to discover that she had lost an arm or leg; finally he realized she was only lacking her children, the three little blondes he always saw her with in town.

"Rebecca Waters," she said, turning to face him. "And you're . . . ?"

Richards spoke his name.

"I've seen you down at the store. You asked me about day care once. You have a beautiful little girl, a brunette with gorgeous eyes. About three years old." Richards nodded, then commented on the surpassing beauty of the woman's own children. They continued in this vein for a while, Rebecca looking boldly, it seemed to Richards, overfrankly right in his face, as if to make a point of how straightforward she was. He began to speak more softly, with his eyes downcast.

Martin, meanwhile, had resumed his position on the edge of the porch. Just as Richards and the woman were running out of things to say, he leapt up with an amazing, gravity-defying movement. Giving Richards a confiding look that stopped just short of a broad wink, he disappeared inside the house. The woman reddened at what she caught of this look. After a moment, she followed Martin inside.

Richards heard sounds of half-suppressed disputation. He tried to catch the drift but failed. Thinking it might be time to leave, he petted the dozing dog, then opened the front door to shout in a farewell. Martin suddenly came back out.

"Don't go yet. Wait a bit. I might need you."

"What for, Martin?"

Now the woman also returned. The color Richards had seen in her cheeks a minute earlier was still there, though less from embarrassment, he guessed, than pique. All three stood around, not knowing quite what to say, till Richards announced that he had better be off pretty soon — it was getting late, and he hated to walk through the redwoods in the dark.

"Yeah, Becky hates it, too," Martin said. "You could take her with you. Don't you hate it there in the redwood forest, Becky?"

"No, not especially. What makes you think so?"

"If you walk down there in the dark, you could trip and break a leg. Then Hank'd get mad at me. He might come up here and punch out my lights, just for fun."

"Oh — are you afraid of Hank now?"

"Not afraid, exactly. Not afraid. But respectful."

This un-self-conscious, if enigmatic, exchange caused Richards to decide once again that it might be time to go. However, Martin took him by the elbow, pressed him down into his broken-backed chair again. There seemed to be no way to escape for the time being.

In fact, Richards wanted to stay; he was curious, eager to witness more of this little contretemps. This unexpected side of Martin, this engaged-with-a-woman side, had interest for him.

Never in the four years of their friendship had Richards known Martin to be "involved" in any way. Martin's air of independence, of backwoodsy self-sufficiency, argued against the very idea of that. Yet he was a handsome, engaging man — a compelling physical specimen. A number of women in the nearby town of Cuervo, as Richards knew from the odd story he'd heard, had thought of him in a romantic connection over the years, and if there was any truth to the rumors, Martin had been party to a number of affairs.

At the Town and Country Tavern, the largest, noisiest, most violent of the four bars in Cuervo, there worked a woman Richards had taken careful note of, a slinky, sardonic redhead who sometimes tended bar, sometimes waited table. This woman had once been Martin's wife. Her small green eyes, dangerously upslanted, were incandescent, shone boldly even in the gloom of the Town and Country, where Richards, as a single man, sometimes repaired for drinks and the hope of companionship. Yet her raw sexiness had an unnerving effect; never had he so much as said hello to her. He had a hard time, for that matter, imagining Martin Declan with such a woman: no two less well suited people came readily to mind, and it was easy to credit the rumors he'd heard of monumental battles, semi-public drunken brawls, staged at regular intervals over the course of their togetherness.

It was easy to imagine the "electricity" they might have generated, too. The woman — whose name, to Richards' disappointment, was the excessively villatic Dee-Anne — was so fulgently female, with the misty, fragrant creaminess of a redhead's complexion confounding her life of daily drinking in smoky dives, that Martin's stalwart male darkness must have seemed her very opposite. All of Cuervo would have held its breath, Richards imagined, would have stood back, as from a depth charge about to detonate, on that night in the Town and Country when they first laid eyes on each other. (In fact, there had been no dramatic, electric first meeting; both had been born in the canyon, had grown up there, had known each other for dog's years.) Indeed, when Richards allowed himself to imagine this woman, he became curiously confused, mentally if not physically weak in the knee; her vulpine beauty was of a sort that spoke to him, piercingly, yet it was also of a sort that caused him to quail, to need to retreat. Such a woman — so flagrant, so delicious an incarnation of female desirability — he shrank from as the self-preserving mortal ever shrinks from the goddess; and he counted himself lucky to know this, to have recognized, in this one situation at least, his own unconditional limits.

Martin, attempting to appear casual, extracted a package of Drum tobacco from his shirt pocket. He soon handed the package to Richards, who also rolled up a smoke. The yellow dog, seemingly asleep, turned its huge head in Becky Waters' direction.

"No," Martin declared, "you'd better not, Becky. You'd better go back. Let Richards here walk you down that nasty path. And if I come to town on Friday, which I might . . . I'll come by. Like the other time."

"No, Martin," the woman immediately replied. "Why would I want that? That's why I came up here. To be at your place this time."

Martin lost steam all of a sudden. He shook his head.

"I've walked those six miles," she continued, "through that damned forest. And before that I had to move heaven and earth just to get away. This isn't just some whim, Martin. This has taken planning. I've worked on this a whole long time, ever since New Year's, in fact."

"I know, Becky. I know you have."

"Do you remember New Year's, Martin? Well, I do . . . I'm not the sort to forget such times. I've got three little children, aged five, four, and two. Remember what you said to me on New Year's, Martin Declan? Do you?"

Martin's head came up. Richards was surprised by the queer, fearful expression on his face, as if he found himself in dangerous waters, yet knew not in what quarter to seek relief. The dog, responding to this sudden movement of Martin's, stirred itself and then, with an expression almost of guilty belligerence, barked once in Becky Waters' face.

Martin immediately grabbed the dog. He hauled it to its feet, pushed it over the edge of the porch. The animal landed on all fours, then quickly took off. A moment later Richards heard it thrashing through the foliage above the house as it forced its way up toward the high ridges.

"I think I'd better go now," Richards said again. He rose from his chair. Becky Waters did not get up to accompany him; nor did Martin urge her to this time.

Two difficult, eventful months passed.

Waking one 6 A.M. to the shrilling of his telephone, Richards took a call from his New York agent, who regretted to inform him that no bids had been received on the paperback rights to his recent novel. Moreover, sales of the hardback edition had been less than anticipated, and he stood in relation to his publisher now as one who has taken payment in advance but who fails to pay back.

Later that same day, thinking to learn the awful truth all at once, if necessary, he called his other agent, in L.A., inquiring about a movie script he had written. The news about the script was also bad, maybe even conclusively bad. Richards hung up and faced the idea that he was now thousands of dollars in debt, with only $700 in the bank and no immediate prospects.

He wandered into his front yard. Like Martin, he lived miles away from any sizable group of other dwellings. The forest began virtually at his front door. There was nothing besides laziness, as it seemed to him, or possibly an exaggerated respect for the law, to prevent him from earning money in the same way Martin did. Martin was now living part-time at Becky Waters' house, on the outskirts of Cuervo. Her husband, Hank, had recently moved out, although sometimes he returned in a semidrunken state, hoping to claim bits of disputed furniture.

With Martin's help, Richards sprouted some high-grade marijuana seeds. At Martin's suggestion, he grew them in cardboard pots, then, under cover of darkness one night, he hauled them up into the woods, to a small meadow near a hidden lake. His plan was to make a garden there, in the open meadow, but Martin assured him that he would lose his crop to human poachers or animal pests. Better to seek out some remote, forbidding place — some inconceivable, inaccessible spot far from all trails. Several days of energetic hiking, through poison oak thickets and along dank creek bottoms, yielded but a single possible site, a rocky ledge high up a canyon wall. This ledge faced to the southwest, which was good, and the soil, though rocky and thin, was probably improvable. A tiny creek ran ninety feet below the garden. Richards would have to haul water all summer, in a backpack rigged to hold five-gallon containers; but he thought he could haul enough if the creek didn't dry up.

Martin, hearing of his plan, warned him not to depend on that creek. It often went dry. Moreover, Richards would be sure to draw attention to his garden, struggling up and down the cliff all summer. Toward the end of the growing season, marijuana thieves roamed the woods, looking for just such signs of unnatural activity. Richards should therefore install a watering system instead, a hidden siphon line running out of some faraway lake or pond. With Martin's help, Richards located, after much frantic searching, a weedy bog only about three hundred yards from his garden. He created a siphon at the deepest point of the bog, then laid down lengths of plastic tubing and buried them. Though this simple system was constantly getting clogged, breaking down in some way, it worked often and well enough for Richards not to have to haul any more water.

By late September, Richards' plants stood over eight feet tall. They were grossly burdened down with resinous marijuana flowers, and by his crude reckoning, they might soon be worth as much as $15,000.

Richards had changed. He continued to write for an hour each morning, but most of his existence was now taken up with thoughts of marijuana, dreams of tax-free marijuana profits, plans for the next year's much larger garden, etc. For the entire summer he was celibate, a virtual monk to horticulture. Few friends came to visit him, sensing his withdrawal, and only his daughter commanded his attention.

He cared for her alternate months now, and those times were inevitably when he most needed to be up in the woods, wrestling with his siphon system, fighting back the wood rats, curing the stem rot that attacked many of his plants. To keep little Margaret occupied, he enrolled her at a day care run by Norma Freel, a pudgy, unjolly woman with four kids of her own. Margaret complained that Norma's house was always cold and smelly, and the eldest of her three sons was sometimes deputized to look over a brood of eight or nine. Richards felt guilty sending Margaret to her, yet his daughter came home looking not much the worse for wear, and so he persisted.

Richards had changed physically, too. His legs had become mightily muscular, and his hands felt capable, like the scarred, knobby extremities of some old farmer. When he ventured into the woods now, it was with an undaunted feeling, as if this were a realm whose measure he had taken, whose secrets he had plumbed. The walk from his house to his garden took forty minutes. At first the trail wound through redwoods, along a clear, cold-running creek; then it climbed and, at a certain tree with a double trunk, headed off through poison oak and stands of bay laurel. Martin had advised against making a single approach to his garden, as this might easily be followed by interlopers. Having found, by a circuitous route, the mouth of the side canyon above which his garden lay, Richards normally traveled the last quarter mile hopping from boulder to boulder along a tributary creek. The point was to leave no footprints, and anything resembling a stranger's mark, any sign of the passage here of persons unknown, was cause for dire alarm.

Martin seemed not to worry, in contrast: he took his precautions, certainly, but for the most part he trusted to a near-clairvoyant sense of what was going on in the woods at any given moment. Though he had never visited Richards' garden, he suggested one afternoon that Richards go "check things out," see if something wasn't wrong up there. The last two nights had been unusually warm, with a discomforting wind blowing down from the high ridges; indeed, Richards found that the fencing around his garden had been completely flattened on one side, probably by some large animal blundering through in the dark.

Though no plants were lost, Richards was deeply disturbed by this incident, and he began to think of the life of the forest at night, the spirits that raged all around his tiny, fragilely defended patch. In a sense, then, it was a miracle each time he returned in daylight to find the work of his confident, perhaps fatuous, human will still undisturbed.

❧

There had been no rain. Richards began to harvest the last week in October, but the bulk of his crop was still on the stalk.

He wore his customary forest uniform: dusty pants, a mud-green shirt, tennis shoes without a tred. In this nondescript outfit he felt nearly invisible, a close ally to the color scheme of the sere, severely faded late fall woods. Going extra cautiously along his creek, he rounded a bend and rested for a moment on a boulder.

Directly below him — so placidly evident as to be unbelievable — was a single footprint. Assuming it to be one of his own, he climbed down off his rock, peered more closely, and almost convinced himself that he had blundered into this sandbank just the other day. But his own shoe left a larger, slightly broader mark, he discovered.

Though Martin had talked to him about this possibility — the steps to take if you surprised someone raiding your garden — Richards couldn't collect his thoughts. His heart pounding, he seemed to recall that there were really only two options: either you confronted the miscreants, made a fight of it (but unfortunately, dope-thieves often came armed), or you backed off, trailed them out of the woods, took revenge later. Martin had lost an entire garden one year to a local man, a notorious drinker and boaster in the Cuervo bars; following a trail of marijuana leaves to the man's cabin, he then simply stole his own harvest back. Thinking of this, of how coolly rational Martin had been in the same situation, Richards was able to still his pounding heart.

Twenty feet ahead of him, the creek went round another bend. He heard a sound from that direction, and he quickly hid in a streamside thicket.

A figure now appeared. Richards stared through the foliage: he was quite unable to accept what he saw, or rather, whom he saw. It was Dee-Anne, the redheaded barmaid; Dee-Anne, Martin's ex-wife, or, possibly, some form or phantom having her shape exactly. She wore black from top to toe. In her right hand she carried an unexpected object, a target-shooting bow made of green fiberglass. On her back was a quiver full of arrows.

Her pale, foxy-featured face, normally focused, acutely expressive, looked vague. Her tendrily hair, bushy, disturbed, rose above her head in a russet cloud. She picked her way along the creek. As she came abreast of Richards' thicket, she stooped to pull a pebble out of one shoe; as she did so, she lost her balance, then hopped to regain it. Turning to her left, she came face to face with Richards' thicket.

For a moment she stared into the foliage. Then with an outraged shout she leapt backward, fell straight back in the rocky creek.

Soon she hauled herself out. But she lay down on the opposite bank, thrashing in the sand. Richards came out of his hiding place.

"Are you all right? I'm sorry. I didn't mean to scare you."

She kept turning, twisting on the ground. Her little bow had fallen some yards off. Richards fetched it for her.

She had fallen on a rock, apparently. Her pants were torn high up the inside of one thigh. A stream of blood ran out of this tear. As soon as Richards saw it, he got a rag out of his knapsack, folded it up to make a compress. Then, without quite thinking what he was doing, he pressed the material between her legs.

"Here. We'll just hold that tight for a minute."

Her strange, tree-green eyes — green like willow leaves — began to flutter. She had raised herself up on her elbows, and as she collapsed Richards put an arm behind her neck. But now he was trapped. With one hand under her, the other holding the T-shirt hard against her crotch, he maintained an awkward position for several minutes.

Finally she came around. Her eyes did not open, but her breathing became more regular. He set her head on the sand.

"That was scary. You'd better not get up just yet," he said. "Stay still."

She brushed his hand away. Without self-consciousness she undid her belt, then maneuvered her pants down below her knees. Her intent was to examine the wound, but its location, far around the circuit of thigh, made this impossible.

"It looks pretty deep," Richards said. "But it's not bleeding much. It may need stitches — I don't know."

She lay back again. Richards noticed the stark whiteness

of her thighs, which were unreal, almost unearthly, in their blank smoothness. Trying not to stare too hard at these remarkable thighs, nor at her bikini-cut panties, he examined her wound more closely.

"You won't bleed to death," he said finally, as if this had been at issue. "All it needs is a tight bandage. You can probably walk out of here."

This encouragement to the contrary notwithstanding, she continued to lie stock-still on the ground. She took hold of his arm, then let go again. Her long neck, arched and vulnerably exposed, attracted his attention: it seemed quite the loveliest neck he had ever seen. There was something classic in its construction. The tender throat, on which a few blond, downy hairs grew, throbbed with an unemphatic pulse.

"Well, I'm kind of thirsty," came the first words from this entrancing throat. "Got anything for me?"

"No. Well, yes," he corrected, "the creek's all right. I drink out of it all the time."

"The creek? This one?"

He formed a cup for her, just like a boy scout, using a waxy leaf. He brought her a drink from the cold creek.

"There's a bug in it," she said. But she drank it all, then asked for more.

Something was happening: though the woman continued to lie still, making no sound, her mood had changed. Richards felt this change in his own chest. Her left hand lay idly across her abdomen, utterly relaxed, as if calling attention to its own repose. She turned her head to look at him. Then she looked away. He became aware, at that moment, of where he was, of the dark forest that surrounded them; of her incomprehensible bow and arrows, lying nearby;

again, of her legs, her pale, elongated thighs. But they were not quite so livid now: even as he watched, they became more pink, more vital. The waxy cup lay on the ground, crushed.

"Have you got a jacket? Something to keep me warm?"

"Yes. I've got an old sweater in my pack."

She asked him to spread it over her, blanket-fashion. As he adjusted it over her hips, she canted her pelvis in his direction, which caused the knee of her injured leg to rise up. But her wound was also changed, remarkably so: it looked smaller than before, and the bleeding had stopped completely. It would certainly not need stitches, he saw. He had been wrong before.

"Your leg looks better. Can you see it?"

She smiled. Her gaze passed back and forth across his face, slowly; he felt that she was looking for something, some sign of "character," perhaps. He became anxious, wondering if she would find it.

Several minutes passed. Richards remained kneeling before her, in a posture almost of worship. The woman touched his hip, looking not quite into his eyes. A strange, thrilling wind blew through the woods.

"No, I don't know where Martin's gone. I haven't seen him in ages."

It was four days before Christmas. Richards had stopped by Becky Waters' house, hoping to run into Martin. In Richards' pocket were several dried marijuana tops, the first smokeable product of his summer's industry. He had hoped to share these with Martin.

"Tell him I don't want to see him anymore," Becky

commanded. "Tell him he's not welcome here anymore. If he wants his stuff, he better come get it. I'll be throwing it out pretty soon."

Richards asked what had happened. All Becky would say was that Martin had been "false": all along, there'd been someone else. Martin cared for someone else, was thinking of someone else. Becky wasn't the sort to accept such a situation.

"I have three kids, you know — a life. I'm not just fooling around here. Martin thinks he can get any woman he wants, but he can't have me, not that way. And he's not such a prize, your friend Martin. He doesn't 'bring it all on home,' if you know what I mean . . . Probably he's up at his cabin, feeling real proud of himself. Looking at himself in a mirror, I'd guess."

The rainy season had begun. Richards' daughter had come down with head lice, and he treated her with a pesticide shampoo, then had to wash everything in his house. That weekend Margaret had a birthday party to go to, and after dropping her off on the coast Richards put on rubber boots and poncho and set off into the woods. The hot, dusty trip to Martin's cabin had become an experience of mud and cold; whole trees were down over the path, uprooted in the recent storm, and the sight of a redwood's massive root clump had an odd effect, depressing and frightening Richards, as if he'd seen the very bowels of some murdered titan. Torrents had washed away the path in places. He edged carefully uphill, keeping always to the steep, steady rise that led to Martin's woodsy hermitage.

The cabin itself looked dark, smashed. Here in Martin's small clearing the wind, imperceptible below, raged crazily in the black, thrashing scrub, and for a moment Richards felt that the storm had had its origin here, in Martin's wild yard. He picked his way across the porch, avoiding several floorboards now missing.

"Martin. Martin — it's me," he called through the open front door.

There came no response. Finally he heard a creaking of springs, as of someone getting reluctantly out of bed.

"I can't see you, Martin. Where are you?"

"Back here."

Richards entered. The house was strangely cold — colder even than the outdoors. Several windows had been left open in the recent storm, and the floor beneath Richards' feet was soaked.

"Martin, I'm just feeling my way. Turn on a light, would you?"

"Come to the bedroom. You know where it is."

Richards at last arrived. Martin then turned on a lamp by his bed; he lay on his side, fully clothed, his shoulders hunched inside a dirty wool hunting jacket. He did not look at Richards.

"Are you sick? What is it?"

"I took a fall. Hurt my back some."

"It smells in here. How long have you been laid up?"

"About a week."

Richards had brought a bottle of Scotch. Martin took hold and drank weakly. He had not shaved in many days — longer than a week, certainly. He had begun to harvest his marijuana gardens just before the storms, he said, and coming down from the ridge one day he tripped on a tree root, fell flat on his back. Something stuck into him.

"God. That sounds painful."

"Yeah, it hurt like bloody fucking hell. I think I passed out."

"Have you got anything to eat? Have you been eating at all?"

"A few cans of soup."

Richards went out to the kitchen, as much to escape the smell of the room as to rustle up food. There were two cans of tomato rice soup remaining, an end of molding wheat bread, and little more. He prepared a can of soup and put a potato in the oven. Back in the bedroom, Martin lay in precisely the same position as before, his eyes closed, his hand grasping the neck of the whisky bottle, which rested on a packing crate. Richards made him sit up in bed. The disturbance of sheets and blankets released an unpleasant odor — Richards almost gagged.

"Christ. You're a mess. I'm giving you a bath."

"No baths. And take that soup out of my face. I want more whisky, that's all."

"Just open your mouth now."

Richards fed his reluctant friend. The bathroom was nearby, and he was relieved to find that there was still hot water. He half-dragged, half-carried Martin in from the bedroom. As Martin undressed, Richards sat on the toilet and tried not to be appalled by what he saw, the mottled greenish skin, painfully bony shoulders, shrunken chest, all this evidence of physical decline. Only Martin's long, slab-like buttocks gave an impression still of resilience, of fleshiness, and the skin of them was deathly marmoreal. His back, however — revealed but for an instant as he slid into the tub — was the most fearsome sight, as there was a wound practically in the middle of it, just to the right of the spine. A roughly circular, freely oozing crust of scab was what Richards saw, and this brief glimpse caused his stomach to turn.

"Your back looks real bad. *Real* bad, Martin."

"What'd you say?"

The hot water had a strong effect. Martin slid under, and when he did not immediately resurface, Richards hurried to plunge his arms in, to pull him out. Martin denied that he had lost consciousness. He'd gone deliciously limp for a moment, that was all; and Richards could let him go now.

"Got all wet, didn't you. Look at your shirt. Here — leave me alone."

"Are you all right?"

"Give me that soap. Might as well get this over with."

One hand drew the bar of soap down a bony, gleaming arm; it seemed to tire before it reached the wrist. Panting, he surrendered the soap. Richards lathered his shoulders, chest, and neck. While soaping Martin's back Richards examined his strange wound, an area of swelling approximately six inches across. In the very center of this swelling was that crusted, diabolical-looking hole, which even now delivered a quicksilver ooze of some sort of greenish stuff. Martin stiffened when Richards probed it. He could not abide to have the swelling touched at all.

"*Real* bad," Richards said again. "You ought to go see a doctor soon."

"Maybe I will. But it's better than it was. At least I'm not pissing blood anymore."

"You were pissing blood?"

Martin took back the soap. He got up on his knees, listlessly soaped his crotch and thighs. But this effort finally exhausted him. He slid back down.

"Martin, what really happened to you? You didn't fall on your back, did you?"

"No," the bather said, smiling.

"Someone shot you, didn't they? I've seen wounds like that before, gunshot wounds."

"No, it wasn't a gun. Some idiot shot me with a bow and arrow, if you can believe it. Right square in the back."

Richards absorbed this astonishing information for a moment.

"A bow and arrow? But what for?"

"How the hell should I know? Didn't even want my pot, either . . . I had a whole gunnysack with me. Just left it there on the path. I woke up and crawled back to the house."

Following Martin's instructions, Richards went into the bedroom and found, in the top drawer of the dresser, a target-shooting arrow, the shaft bent but not broken. Martin had crimped the shaft in the door to pull it out of his back.

"If they were out hunting," Martin said when Richards returned to the bathroom, "they would probably have used triple-bladed points. It was just some joker, I think, running wild through the woods, shooting at anything. And he nearly killed me."

Richards got Martin out of the water. He returned him to his bed, propping him up in some pillows. There were no clean sheets in the house, but at least Martin smelled better now. "If you were pissing blood," Richards opined, "probably your kidney got bruised. It's important to go see a doctor. I'd take you down to the county hospital right now, but I have to get my daughter — she's out on the coast. I'll come back tomorrow."

"All right," Martin said without enthusiasm. "Whatever you tell me, nurse."

Richards remembered the baking potato. He prepared it and urged Martin to eat it. But then there was nothing more to do: he hesitated to bandage Martin's wound, since it clearly needed to drain, and in any case, he could find no antiseptic or gauze in the bathroom cabinets. As he got ready to leave, Martin said, "I'll wait for you tomorrow. You said you'd come back?"

"Yes. I promise." And then Richards added: "You know, I saw someone up in the woods. About a month ago. Someone with a little bow and arrow, arrows just like that one."

Martin remained silent. His eyes were closed, but he was listening.

"Well . . . it was someone you know. It was Dee-Anne — your old girlfriend. She was wandering around my little side canyon, following the creek. I never did ask her what she was up to there. Just taking a walk, I guess."

Martin lay very still. He had sunk far back in the pillows.

"You say you saw — Dee-Anne?"

"Yeah, I even spoke to her. I spent a few minutes with her. Then she went away. But she was carrying a little bow, the kind you buy for $11.95 in a toy store."

Martin frowned. He went limp, just as he had in the bathtub. Richards watched his expression harden; then soften; then harden again. In the end it achieved a suggestive but ambiguous value. Richards was quite unable to read it.

"Dee-Anne? You saw Dee-Anne? And . . . you spoke to her? But did my name come up? Did she mention me?"

"No, not that I remember. She was just . . . there. 'Hunting.' With her funny little bow and arrow."

Richards left shortly thereafter. Evening was approaching, and he could think of nothing more to do. Martin kept hold of the bottle of Scotch, and Richards' last glimpse of him was as he took a long pull. Out on the front porch, the wind was blowing again, gusts from all directions. Clearly a great storm was brewing. Richards glanced briefly at the sky and headed into the redwoods.

He was never to see his friend Martin Declan again. This was their last encounter, there, in the forlorn little cabin, in the lull between two six-day rainstorms. Richards returned early the next morning, but he found the house completely empty, Martin and all his possessions gone. He suspected foul play: Martin's marijuana, which had been drying in the attic, was also gone, and it seemed likely that someone had broken in during the night, then found it necessary to do away with Martin. But the house had been very efficiently looted, utterly cleaned out. All Martin's tools were gone, as were his clothes and books, and the kitchen had been tidied up, the trash buried out back in a pit. The electric power had even been shut off at the pole.

Richards roamed the nearby woods. He could not have said what he was looking for, although he thought of what it would feel like to run across Martin's corpse. He berated himself for having failed to help his friend when he could. Had he taken Martin down that evening, now Martin would be safe, in a doctor's care somewhere. Nor could Richards understand what possibly had possessed him to speak of the questionable encounter with Dee-Anne. Deranged by his own painful memories, a massive feeling of hopelessness and frustration, Martin had more than likely set off into the woods on his own, dragging his pitiful belongings behind him. Becky Waters, to whom Richards spoke about a week later, had heard nothing of Martin Declan. Furthermore, she had just thrown his clothes out with the trash. She was less concerned than Richards about Martin's medical condition, saying that he was "strong as a pig, even when he looks half-dead. The problem with him is he's so sneaky. He always lies."

Richards thought about calling the county sheriffs, but the situation seemed too complicated to benefit from their rough intervention. He continued to roam the wet woods. Late in January, he finally left town for a while to escape the dreadful winter weather, the wettest and coldest in decades. One wild storm, beginning a day after he left, lasted for two weeks and caused massive mudslides to cascade over the Cuervo road, completely isolating the little mountain town. When he returned from L.A., he found his house in shocking disrepair, the roof half deshingled, the water pump shorted out, the driveway flooded. He caught a cold that turned into the flu, and the rest of the winter passed in a fog of discomfort and disease, nothing seeming to work right, relief nowhere in sight.

Not till late April, when the rains finally abated, did he begin to think about Martin again. The path to the cabin would soon be passable; he wondered if by some chance Martin had returned in the night, like some migratory creature reclaiming its tattered nest. No one in town had heard from Martin all winter. There was little concern about his disappearance, which was reckoned just a casual moving on, sure to be followed by an equally casual moving back, as in all the years past. At the Cuervo general store, Richards again ran into Becky Waters, and they spoke agreeably of many things.

"Your children are growing up, just sprouting like weeds. I think they grow better in the rain, don't you?"

"Yeah, probably so . . . Where's your pretty little girl? Not home by herself, is she?"

"She's with her mother now. In Santa Monica. I miss her real bad. It's been pretty grim at the house for a while — a hard winter all around."

"Yeah, well, things are tough. But Hank has a job, have you heard? He's working for the county. Twenty-three fifty an hour. And we're thinking of getting back together. We really might do it."

"Hey, that's wonderful. I'm glad to hear it. Sounds like a smart move."

"Maybe so. I don't know."

Suddenly remembering something else — a piquant bit of gossip, to judge by her expression — Becky pulled Richards away from the store entrance, where others were walking in and out.

"Oh, have you heard, Richards? It's about your old friend. Your Martin Declan — the great woodsman."

Richards looked taken aback, and she continued:

"Yeah, it's pretty strange. Pretty funny, I'd say. He's been found, you know . . . My cousin Carla, who goes to Reno every winter, ran into him. She was at a Safeway when she saw this handsome guy come in, looked like a big gambler, she said. There was just something about him, and then she recognized Martin. He'd grown a mustache. But Carla knows him from years ago. They grew up together, here in the canyon."

Richards looked suitably amazed. But this was good news, certainly: Martin was alive, he was even looking well.

"Yeah, it was Martin. It could only be Martin Declan. Carla thought about saying hello, but something made her shy. There was just something about him. Then he bought some cigarettes and went out, and she lost her chance. But she caught up with him in the parking lot. He was smoking a cigarette, leaning up against a new car. A convertible. And he smiled at her, because he knew who she was. And the girl he was with, a real good-looking Vegas-type girl, also sort of smiled. And then they drove away."

Becky almost winked at Richards: could he guess the rest? There was an air of gloating, of delicious, preening enjoyment of Richards' evident puzzlement.

"You know who it was, don't you? *I* knew — I knew right away. The whole time we were together, like I said, he always had someone else. He was always thinking of someone else. But they couldn't live together, and they couldn't live apart, either. No matter how hard they tried. The usual story, I guess."

Richards still looked bewildered, and Becky admonished him by saying, "Of course you know who I mean. When she heard he'd finally moved in with somebody else, well, it got to her. She just couldn't take that. She always treated him real bad, the whole time they were married. Drinking, fooling around. Running him down. She used to brag she could have any man she wanted in the canyon, and as I heard it, she had quite a few. She's a beautiful girl, I don't take that away from her. But poor Martin. He couldn't get her out of his system. He's got that one weak spot, that one hole in his heart. It might be he'll always have it."

Richards, surprised, reflected that Becky Waters had still not pronounced her rival's name: it was as if she felt there were magic in it, some strange potency best left uninvoked. A few minutes later, he said good-bye to her, but that night he repaired to the Town and Country Tavern, thinking to have a few drinks and also to inquire about a certain someone's whereabouts. Ed Brauch, the owner and keeper of the Town and Country, said that his erstwhile barmaid had been gone since late December. He had had two postcards from her from Lake Tahoe, saying that the skiing was good. But then she always went away in the winter. She came back late each spring.

"I don't think she'll come back this year," Richards opined, happily assuming the role of barstool pundit. "I hear she's living in Reno now. With Martin Declan, in fact."

"Who? With crazy Martin, you say? Are you serious?"

Ed Brauch shook his head in bartenderly disbelief. He reached for his pack of Luckies, then, as if deciding on a healthier course, wiped down the bar with a towel.

"Why Martin Declan, of all people? He only made her miserable. He near drove her out of her mind . . . She's the sweetest, nicest girl, and he just about ruined her life. He always had lots of women, they were hanging all over him, and she only wanted to live a decent life. He broke her heart over and over."

"Well, you know," Richards said, "that's real funny. I heard just the opposite — that she couldn't be true, that she broke *his* heart over and over. I know for a fact she's a terribly jealous person. She followed him up in the woods one day, when he was living with someone else last fall, and —"

"Other way around, my friend — other way completely. *Martin's* the jealous maniac. He was the one always spying and snooping. I saw him beat a man unconscious one night, that was paying her some attention — it happened right here, in front of my bar. Finally she couldn't take it anymore. He scared her. And now she goes back to the guy. You figure it."

"I don't. There's no figuring that sort of thing, is there?"

Stories about Martin and Dee-Anne continued to excite the canyon all that spring and summer. Late in the fall, Richards heard that she was pregnant, and the next spring it was rumored that she had given birth to a boy, a healthy child with flaming red hair. Then a few months later Richards heard that Martin and Dee-Anne Declan had left the city of Reno, though not to return to Cuervo — on the contrary, it was said that they were heading farther away, to Mexico or possibly Montana.

"HEY — ISN'T THAT POMO? YOU KNOW — YOUR mutt?"

Richards, at the town tennis court, had been about to serve to his friend David Chang. It was early in their second set.

"No, it couldn't be. Hey, Pomo! Is that you? Could it be — Pomo?"

Across the road stood a golden retriever of less than the purest breed. It kept trying to mount a smaller animal, a sort of beagle-shepherd mix. When Richards called "Pomo" the retriever looked around guiltily, then got up on two legs again.

Richards laid his racket down and walked off the court. Something about that nervous swivel of dog head, that avid canine grin, I'm about to get some goodies here, oh boy, had hit home, and he had to make sure. The beagle-shepherd mix, not in heat, and not even a female as it turned out, snarled and skedaddled as Richards approached, and the other dog bounded off in pursuit.

"Hey, Pomo! Pomo — come here, boy! Come on — come over here!"

The definite command, voiced loudly, had its effect. The golden turned uncertainly, turned away again, then finally turned all the way around. It slunk forward and, by the time Richards had caught up, was lying flat on its back in a posture of abject surrender.

"Why, I'll be," Richards declared. "I'll be damned for sure. Look at what we've got here. A certain sorry excuse for dogflesh, no doubt about it."

The mad-eyed, panting look of pleasure, as Richards stroked the pink, flea-crossed belly, was confirmation beyond question. David Chang now caught up. He still held his racket.

"I thought so. Just look at that — Why, it's disgusting. Still thinks he's a puppy, doesn't he."

"Yeah, he's got no pride," Richards admitted. "He never had much pride. Oh, Christ," he added as the dog's pink penis, glistening-slick and pointed like a pencil, came out across its belly.

"Look at that," said David Chang. "Some things never change."

Richards hadn't seen his dog in over three years. The very week his marriage ended, Pomo ran away for the last time; it was as if he'd known that the ship of state was sinking, that their little family, one dog plus three humans, would never again be a source of decent grub and warm stove fires.

"My wife left me on a Tuesday," Richards liked to say, "then my dog left, on Thursday. It was a clean sweep."

Pomo — unlike Jackie, Richards' ex-wife — had left him many times before. The merest airborne rumor of a bitch in heat had been enough to make him trot the two miles into town, where, as an adjunct member of the local pack, he besported himself for days on end sometimes. Never a very disciplined pet, despite Richards' vociferous early training efforts, he chased cars, ate the odd unfenced chicken, and always had one rolling eye on the main chance. He hated to be left out, to miss any sort of fun. After his excursions into town he might return in a bloody, half-starved condition; yet he would grin slyly up at Richards as if to say, "Yeah, buddy, but it was worth it — believe me, it was worth every cut and sore."

"I hate to tell you this," David Chang said to Richards over the phone one day, "but your dog's in my back yard right this minute. He's screwing hell out of my neighbor's collie, Lady."

"So?" Richards replied airily. "Let nature take its course, I say. Let the pup have his fun."

"The pup has been having fun since six this morning. Besides, they were going to breed her this time."

"All right. I'll pick him up."

Richards found his dog lying belly down in the grass, his hindquarters chicken-legged to either side. The collie lay a few yards off, her once-proud coat now matted with fluids. Both animals looked utterly spent, but at Richards' approach Pomo got up one last time, as if he knew that the party was about to be declared at an end. The weak, repetitive thrusting of his haunches struck Richards as the most ludicrous thing he'd ever seen, but even so it stung him when David Chang declared Pomo "an inveterate sexhead, pussyhound, and for all I know, a closet Pomosexual to boot."

"Well, I've done my best," Richards replied. "I've tried to set an example of dignity, of self-control. But he's just a dog. He has his drives."

"He has his drives, sure. Everybody has his drives. But look at that face. Something in there knows it's way over the line — and doesn't really care."

❧

Richards had never wanted to own a dog. All through the wild years, the maniac, back-to-the-land days, when people had lived in "communes" there in the coastal hills, he'd resisted the urge, and at times his restraint had marked him as an eccentric. Everybody he knew owned a dog or two; untrainable, oversize mongrels were all the vogue then, great beasts with expressive names like Paw-Paw, Patrice Lumumba, Hardcruiser Mack. Their owners dressed them up in colorful bandannas worn about the neck, and they got taken everywhere, usually in the back of a VW or old pickup. In those days, those wild, organic salad years, to own a dog was to advertise one's robust animal nature, which, despite the majority culture, the workings of the soulless, technofascist insanity then temporarily in the historical driver's seat, had not been fully suppressed. In other parts of the world, robotized white men were dropping herbicides out of helicopter gunships, scorching harmless peasants with flamethrowers; meanwhile, gentle young men and women, exiles to the hills of California and elsewhere, were working a sort of wistful inverse magic, growing their own, refusing to eat meat, recycling cans and bottles.

Richards belonged to this generation by date of birth, certainly. Yet it had taken him a while to get fully synchronized with it. His education, at a top-drawer college full of ironic smarty-pantses, had reinforced in him a tendency to sneer, to stand apart, to point out "logical flaws." He held himself above the fray for a time, but eventually the fun of it all got to him, and he began to prepare for the big upheaval, the cleansing, root-and-branch revolution that they would surely make, which would turn the final page in the world chronicle, ushering in a twilight of the gods and kids. In those beautiful final days, that peaceful ultimate moment, which might last a thousand years, everyone would have enough, the earth would yield up her gleaming bounty, and the gaily caparisoned tribes would all gather round the old wood stove. If he didn't actually believe in this noble vision, Richards thought it wise to proceed as if he did; and he planted his gardens, grew his woolly black hair, and got local.

Even when his first screenplay sold, and he might have lived anywhere he wanted, he stayed in the old, decayed house in the hills. Jackie liked it there, and besides, some value attached to doing this sort of thing on principle. They were young, after all, creative, politically comme il faut; all that had changed was that they now had eighty thousand in the bank.

Jackie was happy, and the scene that grew up around them had everything to do with her countrywoman's ways. In her house people always ate well, listened to good music, never wanted to leave. Richards was more the curmudgeon in the play: deep into his impersonation of the Tortured American Writer, soon he even had a slim novel to his credit. But Jackie welcomed everyone, making life seem something gay, reckless, survivable. Men, especially, liked to get her laughing, eliciting peal after peal from her long, creamy throat. In serious discussion her forehead furrowed sweetly, and she reasoned back and forth, on and on from the same few hardy principles, never losing sight of what was real, what was good and true. Richards came to depend on her for the common-sense approach, the decent, compassionate take on people and situations; and this freed him to be even more outrageous, to court his cranky muse.

He enjoyed his life, in a way, but he was far from content; if not ranting about some literary matter or about the "film biz," which he now presumed to know through and through, he would get onto politics, where his rage was practically bottomless, product of the oppression that he, personally, had perhaps never felt, but that he believed he saw all around him. The world was living with the idea of its own annihilation, he argued, poisoning and despoiling itself, and he took this as a sort of personal affront: it explained why he wasn't really happy, why he felt he had to push and compete, feel slighted at every turn. Meanwhile, he cultivated all the contemporary poses of detachment, the yoga, the talk of karma and dharma, the Buddhist-Hindu-cosmic whatnot. Then by a kind of natural progression, he began to be curious about other women.

In his marriage Richards had experienced from the start a certain "contradiction" (as a radical therapist, hired in a hurry and too late, would later explain it to them). He had wanted to make a decent home, be a good husband, yet his appetites were never quite under control. He was too much of a good boy, though, to be sneaky, even to be very unfaithful; his peculiar way was to secure opportunities, then to refrain nobly, while Jackie had the benefit of feeling insufficient but without being able to rage back, to feel justified in launching mortal counterattacks. But she was infinitely sensitive here, strangely without faith in her remarkable beauty; something had happened back in the bosom of the family, back beneath the roof of the rambling, Toad Hall–ish manse that the Featherwell family still maintained outside Darien, Connecticut, where old Adam Featherwell, hard-drinking patriarch and prodigious earner, had once spanked her too hard. Or too long, or something like that. It was indicative, perhaps, of Richards' inability to focus on anyone other than himself for more than a moment that he had never quite gotten his own wife's story straight, and he persisted till the end in thinking that his hardy abundance of urge was all they really needed.

In other ways, though, they were quite well suited. Richards loved her — really loved Jackie, in his way. Who could help but love her; it was like loving blue sky, ripe apricots, an early rain. He loved her, yes, but a vagabond calling herself Sparrow after an illumination during a bird-themed acid trip came to their house one summer, and when Jackie went off to visit Mom and Dad on the coast of Maine, the nasty thing actually happened. And Richards frankly enjoyed it. But he was made for this, he suddenly saw: by nature he was a lover, *ein Sammler von Frauen,* and for such a man there could be no crude restrictions. No, he had a broad swath to cut, a memorable life to live, not only as a man, but as that most privileged sort of being, a *writer.*

One might even say that he had a responsibility in this regard. And then Jackie came home, sensing something amiss, and he quickly confessed. Not abjectly, not even guiltily — only hastily, as if he wanted to get this silly matter out of the way.

Jackie took the news in silence. She did not protest, did not rage or break down. It would take her six years to get her own back, but in that moment their marriage was already over, they were doomed. Sensing accommodation, Richards coolly inquired if Sparrow might be allowed to stay another few days. Jackie still said nothing; showed nothing.

In the end, the bird-girl stayed till the next spring. And when she finally left, dragging her dusty wings a bit, Richards was heartily glad to see her go. But for a certain sort of man, this was only to be expected — to live under one roof with two tortured, jealous women, this was nothing special, for a certain sort of man.

Had he really acted this way? Had he been that awful thing, a sexual bully, greedy, unthinking, insulting? When he got around to totting up the accounts many years later, after his wife finally left him, he found that he had overspent grossly, had fallen badly into debt. From a distance his figure had a disturbing, even frightening, aspect; and for the first time he felt ashamed.

But the times, the times — ah, surely their "era" explained it all. To have been afoot in those days was a kind of bliss, truly, but to have been young, this was indeed an invitation to insanity. They had conspired to jettison everything, he later came to believe, to rid themselves of all customs and standards, anything by which they might be called to personal account. They were a generation determined not to judge themselves, mad for pleasure, avid for strong, undisciplined sensation. Of course, things hadn't really been like that, not in the day-to-day of most of the people he knew, even the most outlandish among them. An ordered, conventional existence had gone on in the midst of all the madness, behind various screens. But the context, the cultural background noise: this, indeed, had been monolithically orchestrated, he later realized, omnipresent, insidiously influential. He himself had been nothing like a serious practitioner of "free love," of course — he with his mincing, middle-class fear of real uncleanness, his need for tenderness, respect, faithfulness from a spouse. But the times had encouraged him in a certain direction, and he had wanted to see what he could get away with.

Jackie had never been unfaithful, not with another man. Somehow he had knocked the stuffing out of her even to that extent, and when she finally got up the nerve to leave, the gross asymmetry of their relation made the parting irreversible. If she had kept step along the way, he sometimes thought, accumulated her own little book of secrets, they might have patched things up. But she had been honest, caring, respectful: in all important ways, a good wife.

The final blow, he could see now, came in the year before their daughter was born, when a friend of Jackie's, a "sister" from one of her women's groups, came to live with them for a while. Gudrun was another resident of the canyon, and she had recently bought a cabin that needed to be remodeled. She asked to stay while the second story was added on, and though Richards hesitated to take in yet another houseguest, Jackie insisted. In her early years, G.

(as she liked to be known) had been a well-regarded folk musician, a charter member of a lively, semifamous scene back east. She was a good piano player, an adequate guitarist and mandolinist, and her windy, colorful voice sometimes yielded beautiful effects. Tall and plump, with fragrant, dusky skin she credited to a black ancestor, she was dauntingly serious of mien, always under some sort of cloud; in that age of glib acceptance she was often frankly intolerant, and Richards perversely admired her for this. She arrived for her stay of a week with a worrying amount of luggage. Two and a half months later, everyone concerned agreed that she might as well stay the whole winter, since the contractor had bungled the foundation work on her house, and they hated to think of her living in an off-kilter kitchen. Besides, she was happy with them; she declared Jackie to be her best friend, and Jackie felt constrained to issue the expected counterpronouncement, that G. was also *her* best friend, that she now had a sister closer than her own real sister. The winter passed in disgustingly earnest felicity.

Richards had never fancied her, and the ménage they formed was of the most innocent sort, two women being strong and "supportive" with each other while the husband showed all due respect, etc. But Richards liked to hear G. sing and play, and one night they drank some wine and she shifted into a new mode, and the silvery tune she tickled on the piano, with fingers that seemed surprised at their own dexterity, went straight to his heart. Thereafter he found her attractive, especially her skin and her small, black-olive-colored eyes, which would only look sidelong at him, amused to see that she had won another one, made another musical conquest; just the tiniest crack appearing in his facade of stalwart, good-fellow husbandhood, and she, too, was changed, although later he came to think that she had had an "interest" all along. But he did nothing about this new feeling, and in fact the path to consummation took a devious, perhaps original turn. In their women's group Jackie and G. had often discussed the possibility of a Sapphic attachment — it was good, it was au courant, and each confessed that though she wasn't really inclined that way, if she had been, surely it would have been toward the other. Now G. reintroduced this exciting notion. It was four months since she'd come to live with them; in that period, she had had no lovers, and it occurred to Jackie that the purpose behind her stay, the actual motive underlying all this intense, uncommon befriending, was to promote what she claimed to have no real taste for. Perhaps G. *did* have that taste, truly was inclined. It had only taken her a while to get up the courage.

The two women became uncomfortable then; still the best of pals, ostensibly, still mouthing the catchphrases of their approved comradeship, they circled warily, began to speak as if hearing undertones in all they expressed. Richards had been given a puppy, a tawny fluffball destined to grow into the undisciplined, absurdly oversexed Pomo. He took his new pet out for walks some days, and one afternoon he returned to find the house in an atmosphere of crisis. G. was already upstairs, angrily packing. Jackie was moping around in the kitchen, almost in tears. Then G. came down, and she had been crying. Thinking to act the conciliator, the Esalen-style feelings facilitator, Richards put his arms around both of them, pulling them close. G. began to sob, and she blurted out that she was entirely at fault, the whole problem was that she cared too much, she loved Jackie too, too much. This group embrace turned into a clinch between the women alone, with Richards pushed unceremoniously off to the side.

Love shall find a way . . . Two hours later G., who had retreated upstairs with Jackie, came down again. She took Richards by the hand and led him into his bedroom. Here she confessed that she had just made love to his wife — she hoped he didn't mind, and since they wanted to hurt no one, to leave no one out in the rain, Jackie had just "given" him to G. for the afternoon. The oddity of this situation was sufficiently interesting, sufficiently compelling in itself, but the more Richards thought about it, the more he liked the idea of being "given," traded around like an Eskimo wife. Three days later, they all went to bed together, and thereafter, on a regular basis. The two women were the main attraction, supposedly, with Richards thrown in just for spice, but he didn't mind; there was an agreeable sensation of getting up to speed, of finally living the way all those crazy-assed, long-haired hippies were supposed to, up there in their loosey-goosey communes.

G. was happy, Jackie also seemed happy, and Richards was once again fatuously content to have more than he wanted. Certain men were destined to live as they chose, he realized: not as society required, but simply as they wanted, according to their own rules. One of these rules, he decided, was that no one was ever to feel excluded, and Jackie and Richards went so far as to take their new lover on their vacation that year, a backpacking trip to the Sierras, where they camped and fished and lay naked for hours in the sun.

Despite what was to happen among them later, Richards could never make himself regret that piquant interlude, with its surfeit of ease and lascivious play, the women lying sun-browned out on the boulders, and Richards, like some primordial squaw-man, going first to one, then to the other, the sun beating on the tomtom of his youthful backside. Along the banks of the Middle Fork they achieved a sexy, tripartite union, he felt — it did not feel foolish at the time.

Once, G. pulled him into the bushes, and with a look of joy that was almost frightening, she confessed that she was madly in love, deeply, entirely in love with him. It was the sort of declaration that required a response, and after a moment he said, "But I thought it was Jackie you loved. Isn't it really Jackie?"

"No. Don't you know? Haven't you always known?"

Thereafter, he felt uneasy sometimes. They swam together in the cold green pools of the river, but he did not wash clean, he did not emerge refreshed. He began to look at his wife in a new way, seeing her as someone already half lost to him, because her lovely, decent shoulder bones, as they showed in her bare back, had been entrusted to him, given into his care, and he had not acted to protect. He had never before noticed (at least not consciously) how really young she was, how like a woodland bird or butterfly, animated by a pure, sweet spirit, incomparably swift and bright. The massive boulders down by the river, among which she gracefully flitted, were like the forces of life itself, of ponderous, killing fate, and she was as nothing compared to them. Feeling him stare at her moodily, she asked if his stomach was hurting again, did he want another cup of peppermint tea.

"No. I'm all right. But come over here, why don't you. Give us a little kiss."

"Maybe I will."

As he held her, kissing her with sudden passion, he felt that she was already gone from him — he sensed doom in the situation, and he was saddened, afraid. Even so, he could think of nothing to do about it right then, nothing to say; the feeling of dread just flickered on and off, did not compel sufficiently. When she walked away, showing him her superb, womanly backside — and those shoulder bones, the subtle, tender blades, where mystic wings invisibly attached — he felt it piercingly again, all the pointless pain and loss.

"You're very beautiful," he said softly. "Especially from behind."

She turned to look at him, not at all coyly. "I should think you'd had enough of that by now . . ."

The dénouement was swift, crazily harsh. Something happened between the women that Richards didn't witness, fateful words were exchanged. Within a month it was known that they were deadly enemies. G. sent Richards a letter, urging him to leave his wife. He replied in the negative. Two years later, in the midst of his divorce, Jackie herself sent Richards a long letter, containing a copy of something she had written at her therapist's suggestion, a compendium of his marital transgressions. About the affair with G. it had this to say: "You wanted her all along, just as you wanted everybody, because you could attract them. But you didn't have the guts to do it, not on your own, so you dragged me in. I hate you, and I feel ashamed for you, deeply ashamed. She saw she could get to you through me, because she saw you didn't care enough about me to stop it, and you didn't mind if she used me that way. I still have the taste of her cunt in my mouth. Whatever happens to me in my life, I won't ever let someone pretend he loves me again."

Tennis. Richards, his mind not really on the game, hit a lucky drive that put him up 5–4, with his serve to come. But he suddenly didn't feel like playing anymore.

"You're quitting? Just like that?" asked his friend David Chang.

"Yeah. I'm depressed. It was seeing that mutt, Pomo. Seeing my stupid dog again."

After a brief petting, the dog had run off once more. They could see him even now, outlined on the crest of a nearby hill. He was sniffing the tail of a small brown animal, possibly a cocker spaniel.

"He'll get shot someday," David Chang ventured. "By an irate dog-husband, if I don't miss my guess."

"You know — they call him Zuma now," Richards replied. "It was on his dog collar. I guess it's just as well that somebody took him in. He's got a new home and all."

Rackets in hand, they walked up to Chang's house. His new wife, Joanne, was a nurse at the hospital where David ran the emergency room, and she served them dark beer and pistachio nuts. Sitting out on the deck of the house, watching a long-lived sunset of aquarelles, Richards couldn't stop thinking about his dog; he wondered if he ought to try to reclaim him, find the presumptive owners and dispute their claim to title, take the philandering prodigal back into the fold.

"Naw, just forget it," David Chang opined, "it's all

over. He's part of your past, man, and you can't ever go back. When Merle and I split up" — Merle was Chang's first wife — "I thought I'd keep the house, keep the dogs, but I was wrong. I only got free of it when I gave it all up. Besides, he's a miserable, no-account animal. You saw it again today — there's something wrong with him. He's got sex-for-brains. I'm not kidding, he's a sicko, from way back."

Richards smiled, but in his heart he felt a great, nameless longing. If only he could get his hands on that dog, start over from the beginning, with a better system for training, perhaps, he might work wonders. Instill a sense of self-control, which had always been the problem — a modicum of doggish decency. He couldn't turn the clock back, he had lost his precious beginnings, he now knew; but still he wanted to see his dog, get hold of him for just a while.

RICHARDS STOPPED GROWING MARIJUANA WHEN his daughter became old enough to identify the plants. She would say to visitors, "Daddy doesn't grow pot in the front yard anymore 'cause it might get ripped off, so he grows it up in the woods," which was true. He could imagine the time when she would display her precocious knowledgeability to the wrong person, but even more he was troubled by the thought that he was storing up a disaster, that one day, say when she was sixteen, he would tell her not to do something and she would laugh in his face. His last season of growing was when she turned four. He sent six pounds to his brother on Maui, then sold another six or seven himself. It was 1981, and seedless tops of good quality brought $2,000 per unit.

He had had a good run, had never been arrested or

robbed at gunpoint. One of his early gardens, built too close to the house, had been discovered by local teens and picked clean, but otherwise he'd always harvested what he planted. Besides, he'd enjoyed himself. He liked learning about the plant, with its intricate character and manifold properties, he'd conducted multigenerational, Luther Burbank–ish experiments to produce yet more potent strains, and he'd explored all the local canyons, looking for choice sites to cultivate. The time he spent in the woods, in the poison oak thickets and blackberry tangles, had never felt wasted; on the contrary, he'd valued the outdoor work, the chance to become a simple laborer, at one with the soil.

His mentor in the business had always been the elusive, mysterious Martin Declan. But Richards' true confederate was his brother-in-law Terry, also known as T.R., Jackie's youngest brother of three. When Richards quit growing, T.R. kept right on, and the next year he made over $40,000. He liked to say that even more than the money, he enjoyed the taxes he didn't have to pay.

A con man, charmer, and bad seed *extraordinaire,* Terry had lived with Richards and his wife almost from the start of the marriage. When Richards first visited the Featherwell family home, on many acres outside Darien, he found Jackie's younger brothers living together in an attic room; they were grown men, handsome, not unintelligent, but they seemed to spend all their time lying in bed smoking pot, drinking beer, and trading quips. Terry had been expelled from a number of boarding schools. Brat, the older brother, had actually gone to college for a while; he read hundreds of books a year, sometimes six or seven a week, science fiction and military history, mostly, and he'd taught himself to play the electric guitar in a slashing, faster-than-the-speed-of-light style. He stuttered badly and seemed utterly lost. When Richards offered both of them a place to stay, should they ever come out west, only T.R. responded, saying he just might show up someday.

That was in the spring of 1971. In July Terry arrived with a girlfriend and all his worldly belongings, everything jammed in the back of a Volkswagen minibus, in the approved contemporary style. A lot of people were living at Richards' house just then: some stayed only a week, some a year or more, not necessarily in the house proper, but in the domes, yurts, lean-tos, and tipis scattered over the woodsy property. Terry went scouting up in the forest, and when he found a spot he liked, he quickly built a platform out of scavenged plywood. When Richards first saw the rude, altar-like platform, something stirred in him, and he felt that he, too, would probably rather be sleeping out under the starry night; a certain authority and taste, a negligent sort of inspiration, were evident just in the way the hunks of wood had been tossed together. Thereafter, he often noted the squalid glamour of the places his brother-in-law occupied, a Gypsy-encampment sort of feel; everything was transformed by T.R.'s touch, both degraded in some indefinable way and made more interesting.

In personal style he was equally perplexing. It took Richards some years to realize that he loved his brother-in-law, that he also hated having him around, that life at the house was both better without him and more forgettable. All Terry had learned at those boarding schools was how to look self-possessed no matter what, and his cynicism about work, the straight world, friendship, loyalty, life itself, though rarely expressed (and always sweetly, amusedly), was profound, to the extent that any attitude of youth can be profound. He was a larger, darker, stranger version of his sister, Jacqueline, her masculine counterpart. Sister and brother did not dote on each other, exactly, but they were extremely closely bound, with the loyalty of two pups from the same unhappy litter, each knowing the oldest, deepest wounds of the other. In each case Dad Featherwell seemed to be the prime baleful influence: for Jackie it was a question of love inexplicably withdrawn, at just the point when she began to mature, and for T.R., who had never felt the paternal warmth at all, a blanket disapproval beginning at the moment of birth. But Richards had to rely on Jackie for this imprecise analysis: Terry never spoke of his father, never tried to account for his own problems in any systematic way.

Most likely, he felt he didn't deserve to be explained; a good deal of his charm lay in this, in a wistful refusal to presume, to lay claim to one's analytic attention. For several months he hovered at the edges of Richards' scene, always cool, always reserved, seemingly bemused. When approached he would respond, generally in a friendly manner; but he needed no one, it was clear, he trusted no one. Richards engaged him cautiously, and over time he came to adopt Jackie's attitude toward her brother, which was to ask little and expect less, and on this basis it was possible to get along with him, even to become fairly good friends. Both of them were avid tennis players, after all; and on some trips into the Sierras, where they fished and camped in wild, stony canyons, they discovered other compatibilities, each of them tending toward the Neanderthal in matters of equipment, attitude, approach.

Richards liked to take drugs in those days. One of his fondest pleasures was to go up into the mountains, far off the ordinary backpacker tracks, and make a rude camp; he would bring little in the way of supplies, just a sleeping bag, a pot, a knife, and some matches, and one feature of these adventures was always a dose of some exotic brain chemical or other. His interest in "psychedelics" had started back in college, back in the days when the great enlighteners themselves, Leary and Alpert, were touring the eastern campuses, describing their epochal experiments and coincidentally bringing around some drugs for distribution. Following an appearance at Richards' little college, when the future Ram Dass boldly claimed that a single dose of LSD-25 produced a sensation equivalent to "fifty or sixty good orgasms, maybe more," Richards became enamored of the idea, and he began an acquaintance with mind manifesters that was to continue for fifteen years. But he was a cautious, self-protective kind of drug pioneer. He never took too much, and he always inquired into a sample's purity and provenance, ensuring himself as best he could of a sunny, larky experience. The Sierras in high season were almost always sunny, he found, and he liked nothing better than to lark about in the alpine meadows, with Jackie or Terry in tow, their minds made utterly ridiculous by the clarity of sky and lake water. After a brisk hike to the crest of some distant hill, which had seemed a virtual Everest when glimpsed in the blue-scented dawn, Richards might turn to his young wife and notice that her face was horribly wrinkled, seamed and withered like a hunk of fallen pine.

"Cowboys," he might say to her, thinking to express thereby some enormous body of thought, of sensation and integral understanding. "Clouds and blue cowboys, sort of."

And the beautiful, frightening young crone, her nose gone iridescent, would join him in gut-wrenching laughter, just as if she knew what he was talking about.

Acid and mescaline, pot, peyote, and yohimbine bark; morning glory seeds (only the "Heavenly Blues"), psilocybin, hashish, and Moroccan kif; coca leaf; betel nut; *amanita muscaria,* the red-topped mushroom known as the Destroying Angel; yage; Hawaiian woodrose. Lei-lei root. A milky fluid made from hard red beans, Peruvian in origin, that caused them to hallucinate in ripples for hours. This in brief was Richards' psychoactive diet, the mental menu of his youthful days and years. The idea of killing off a few brain cells, a likely consequence of such indulgence, was positively attractive to him, since he felt that he had gone too far in the opposite direction, into logical mentation, and he was hoping to begin to relax, to "evolve." He found more to admire in the photos of the Stone Age Tasaday people, recently discovered in a Philippine rain forest, than in all the piano concertos of Mozart, so brittle and overwrought, or in the modern philosophy he had once liked to read, or in the chess problems that had been his bedside amusement for years. The Tasaday, shown squatting under gigantic, shiny leaves, which they used for clothing as well as shelter, sat out rainstorms lasting whole weeks, so content were they with the wordless, meaningless pulse of their primitive group consciousness. Lost in an eternal present, they had no need of books, art, gadgets, or argument; they owned nothing, only the ringing, permanent moment. And this was enough.

He had more to learn from them, or from his pet cat, which could sit for hours by the wood stove, boldly, purringly alive, than from all the sages and logic choppers he had once revered. Talk itself was a mistake, he believed, since talk necessarily followed thought, and thought of the sequential sort was his culture's deepest curse, the source of its hateful pathology. For a period of several years he shared, or felt he shared, a specific understanding with about ten million other people, all of them roughly the same age, of similar background, all similarly disaffected from the mainstream. In politics they were "radical," differing only in the degree to which they embraced, from positions of little risk, violence as a means; in culture they generally admired resentful, earthy expressions, nothing too complex or refined; in spiritual feeling they shrank from all that was established, conventional, comprehensible, American. The world underculture, which probably exists in all times, in all locations, waiting only to be granted the credence it can never earn on its own, burst forth for them in colorful, subversive array. Ouspensky and Blavatsky; foot reflexology; Jethro Kloss, the high priest of the "high enema"; macrobiotic food. Gurdjieff and Meher Baba, not to mention the eye-rollings of Sri Chinmoy. As a chronic allergy sufferer, Richards gave up pills and inhalers overnight, and so great was his desire to be cured, such his newfound commitment to earth-grown, organic goods, that he found some herbs that seemed to do him good. Likewise, he came to see that mental distress was bodily in origin; his own mind, that flawed, unhappy thing, locus of shameful images and reductive processes, nothing more, could be refreshed by the manipulations of chiropractors, Rolfers, and the odd Alexander or Feldenkrais man.

Were other people feeling what he was? That a great new idea, an epochal illumination, was just now taking form, and that they were its exemplars, one might even say its avatars? Indeed, many people were. This new idea, and the feeling that he, himself, was helping bear it along, rode in tandem with Richards' use of all those many drugs, although in periods of relatively undrugged consciousness he still felt that they were on to something, some fresh understanding of how to be. On his twenty-sixth birthday, he took a whopping dose of acid and hiked up into the hills by himself, to a green, weedy pond he loved. Here he swam by himself all day. He did not achieve an ecstatic oneness with the macrocosm, a piercing, transfiguring identification with trembling space; it was more of an ordinary, so-what-else-is-new kind of revelation, of the blissful friendliness of time, into which he fit exactly. His wife had baked a birthday cake in his absence, chocolate both inside and out. The cake was so perfectly itself that he wept at the sight of it; but he couldn't eat any, the acid wouldn't let him.

In 1974, when his brother-in-law had been living at his house for three and a half years, Richards finally got up the nerve to ask him to leave. No problem; and as soon as Terry was gone, Richards and his wife began to get along much better. They had grown used to the shadowy, semiparasitic presence of her brother, the psychic weight of him; T.R. was a quantity always to be considered, pondered in some anxious corner of the heart.

He wasn't gone long. When he returned from Mexico, only four months later, Richards and Jackie welcomed him, despite their recent relief at his departure. He had written several long letters home. (According to Jackie, these were the first written communications anyone in her family had ever received from him.) He described the foliage on the coast of Quintana Roo, the crustaceans he ate when he ran out of money, a certain fishing adventure off the Belizean coral reef. Richards admired these letters sincerely. He believed they were addressed primarily to him, since they were full of a flavorful factualness that Terry knew he valued. He went so far as to say that they reminded him of *Sketches from a Hunter's Album,* in particular, of the story "Bezhin Meadow," which he'd once gotten his brother-in-law to read. He was hearing, in these letters, from the "real" T.R., he felt, from a sensitive, vulnerable soul previously kept under wraps. (Upon hearing his epistolary style praised so fulsomely, Terry seemed embarrassed: the thing about traveling, he said, was that it sometimes wasn't boring.)

After a brief stay with Richards and Jackie he moved to San Francisco, where some friends had rented a house on Stanyan Street. Here he stayed for half a year, enjoying the company of his old prep school pals. One of these well-funded ne'er-do-wells, a boy named Borden Pullman Biddle, had recently come into a world-class inheritance. There were many parties, good times all around.

One evening, the San Francisco contingent, with Borden Biddle at the wheel of an old Jag sedan, came hurtling up Richards' driveway, laughing, hooting, tossing bottles just to hear them smash. Once inside the house they revealed other bottles of a truly venerable Cognac, but they retired upstairs, to Terry's old bedroom, without offering Richards so much as a sip. Two hours later he was standing in an ice-cold shower, helping to revive Drake, one of the madcap revelers, who had taken too much morphine sulfate on top of all that good brandy. The poor, blue-skinned fellow was hardly breathing anymore, and they had to walk him outdoors to bring him around.

"Terry — they don't shoot up, do they?" Richards asked the next morning, when the prep school lads had departed. "They don't geeze and spike, and all that — they aren't junkies, are they?"

"Junkies? Oh, no — I wouldn't say so. Maybe some of them use from time to time, but as a general rule, no. I wouldn't think so."

"Well . . . even so, I don't want them coming around. It wouldn't be pretty if some young Rockefeller was to croak in our toilet, if you see what I mean. Might be hard to explain."

"All right. Fair enough."

Thereafter, Terry stayed in the city only part-time; possibly he had taken Richards' suggestion, or maybe he had only exhausted his urge to party. In the end he even had a few disparaging things to say about Borden Biddle, who had begun to act the lord with all the others.

Over the next year and a half, Richards came closer to his brother-in-law than ever before, and at the same time, he came closer to wanting to kill him. The big mistake was to have ever loaned him money; it was something you didn't do with a brother-in-law, not if there was any way around it, and though the sums themselves were fairly small, the sum of the sums was not, by Richards' modest standards. Far from showing any gratitude, T.R. seemed to resent having to pay back, and this bone of contention was to be chewed between them for a long time. Terry decided, after his brief sojourn in Mexico, that he would try to be a writer: he saw no reason not, since he seemed to have some talent. (Richards often had this effect on friends;

seeing his success, the outflow from so flawed and unremarkable a vessel as he, they felt encouraged, as if anyone might then learn the simple trick.) In self-conscious imitation he now sat down in front of a typewriter each morning, just like Richards, then proceeded to hunt and peck morosely for a few hours, in the end producing many beginnings of things. Richards read whatever he was shown, and he prescribed large doses of Crane, Faulkner, Hemingway, and the beloved Russians, not just Turgenev, but Chekhov, Pushkin, Tolstoy, Goncharov, Leskov. He conducted a sort of class, Jackie sometimes also sitting in, after Terry had struggled through most of *Lolita* and the first two chapters of *Speak, Memory* at Richards' suggestion. There were gaps in his background, to be sure, substantial educational deficits, but these could always be made up. And then there was the evidence of those wonderful letters, those surprising bits of toothsome color sent back from Mexico.

"Anyone who can write that shark-hunting scene," Richards assured his brother-in-law, "can write other things, too. Really good things. It's just a question of making yourself come awake: of letting life play on you, like on guitar strings. Nabokov is major league vibrating guitar string, if you see what I mean . . ."

This pedagogical adventure ended soon enough. Richards saw that he had no real talent for instruction, nor did Terry, a reluctant Galatea at best, really want to learn. He lacked the reserves of confidence, the ready adjustment to self-disgust, that Richards believed was necessary in someone trying to write something good each day. In 1976, he abruptly sold his typewriter, then began to grow marijuana in earnest, enough to earn him a comfortable living. (He had no real expenses, Richards was prone to note, no rent to pay, no grocery or insurance bills, although Jackie did require him to pay for his beer, two six-packs a day in warm weather.) With some money in his pocket for once, Terry quickly recovered his self-respect, and an old girlfriend, Lonnie, came to live with him again. But then Lonnie abruptly departed after only a few days in residence. Terry claimed not to care very much: as always, he had many romantic irons in the fire.

Now twenty-five years old, Richards' brother-in-law was a good-looking, sexy man, tall, black-haired, with a knowing smile and dark, devilish eyes. The old English ballad "Black Jack Davey" never failed to remind Richards of T.R.: like the song's subject, he had a talent for audacious, lightning-fast seduction, and he almost always got away with everything:

Last night I slept in a warm feather bed
Beside my husband and baby
Tonight I'll sleep on the cold hard ground
In the arms of Black Jack Davey
In the arms of Black Jack Davey.

The women he attracted — over the years, there were dozens — understood from the start that he was a "bad" one, someone to be enjoyed just for a little while, gone a little crazy over, not held to strict account. Sometimes, he fell in love himself, and he was capable then of suffering much like anyone else. But these instances were rare. Lonnie, the girlfriend who had come and gone, exercised a particular hold over him lasting several years. Richards had never really liked her; he found her remarkably selfish, and with a ready litany of justifications for being so. But she was clear-headed, smart, and usually right about things, and he paid close attention when she said of her own boyfriend, "Terry wants to be good, but he wants to be bad just a little bit more. He'll come to a sad end."

What this "end" might be, Richards hardly bothered to imagine. They were too young to be thinking about sad outcomes, certainly; and in the meantime, Richards was struggling in his own life, sensing his marriage begin to fail, losing the thread of his writing. Only occasionally did he worry about his brother-in-law, who, in early '78, finally moved out of the house for good (the proximate cause was the birth of Margaret). He moved only a few miles away, to another old farmhouse colonized by long-haired youth. Here he began to grow pot in greater quantity, in gardens hidden away in the forest; and he came to depend less on his sister for emotional coddling, less on Richards for loans and companionship. When they met at the tennis court now, they exchanged news, wisecracks, and volleys in much the old manner; but there was a feeling, on Richards' side at least, of having missed an opportunity, a chance for some deeper connection. Seven years of living together, of being in each other's hair, brothers of a kind, partners in crime: it should have led to something more, really should have. They had taken all those drugs together, after all.

"Terry — I heard from Arnie Dittman today. He's back from Bolivia. I don't know how he managed it, but he brought back three hundred coca cuttings. Wants to plant them up on our ridge, make us a little plantation."

"Oh, I don't know," came the mild-mannered, drawling reply. "Cocaine's sort of stupid, don't you think? It's a bullshit type of drug. That's why all these dentists and accountants like it so much . . . makes them feel real 'bad,' you know."

They had taken mescaline together dozens of times; they had given great doses of LSD to each other, using it to fuel manic treks high in the mountains, "vision questing" and all that. Maybe there were other cultures where young men induced weirdness, instability, and frightening vulnerability in each other, sought a kind of spirit-brotherhood but using nobler, nonchemical means; maybe there were, but this was their own flawed culture, their own corrupted world, and these were its faulty materials, this its only moment in time. Maybe their "experiments" would one day come to seem factitious, their so-called revelations just so much erratic brain-wavery; but for the time being, absent other modes of transfiguration, this was what they had.

"T.R., I got a bag of mushrooms this morning. It came via UPS. No return address, and no note inside."

"But you know who sent it, right?"

"No. Not really."

The mushrooms were unattractive. They were squashed, smashed, barely identifiable as organic matter. They might have been any sort of debris sealed inside a Vac-Pac.

"Might be deadly poison," Terry noted wisely. "A true poison-pen package. I wouldn't eat even a stem of it. Not on your life."

" 'When early man,' " Richards immediately quoted, having readied, for just this purpose, one of their favorite texts, a sententious volume justifying all manner of drug abuse, " 'when early man first encountered the hallucinogenic plant, he met at that moment the pure unknown. A strange shape, an unlikely material, for instance, one of the New World puffballs, order *Gasteromycetes,* would have offered him scant inducement to ingestion. Nevertheless, over the eons primitive man came to sample everything. Should we conclude, therefore, that our forefathers roamed the ancient deserts, meadows, and forests in search only of physical sustenance, or rather, should we say that, from a very early date, our ancestors recognized the . . . trembling mystery of corporeal existence, a mystery made manifest, lucid, and briefly endurable through the agency of precisely those "unlikely materials"? . . . Furthermore, the idea of a deity may have first been suggested by such substances, for example, by *Psilocybe caerulescens* var. *nigripes,* known among the Mazatecs as "the mushroom of superior reason." In the Old World, too, we see that the ritual use of mind-manifesting materials predated the development of polytheistic religious practice, which indeed, it probably called into existence . . . From the point of view of the ancient peoples, then, the world existed largely to *provide* these substances, to throw them in the path of questing souls, the primal explorers of human consciousness. The more uncommon, the more repulsive a substance, the more likely its utility as . . . another source of the flashing rapture . . .' "

"Ah — that old flashing rapture, indeed," Terry said. "That crazy, wacky flashing rapture, which I dearly know and love."

"Yes, and don't forget this, either: 'the more uncommon, the more repulsive.' I think what we have here is sufficiently repulsive, wouldn't you say, T.R.? Disgusting enough to justify all manner of experimentation? Well, what about it — is it 'uncommon' enough? 'Unlikely' enough for you?"

"Oh, it's definitely unlikely. Could be the mushroom of superior reason, its own self. Wouldn't surprise me at all."

In the end, they split the package in half, eating every stem and top. Then they flew away for about twenty hours. Superior reason did not result — if anything, it was galumphing, rampaging unreason that came to visit them, antireason pulsing in the very walls.

But those were the good times, the bright and hopeful days; with any luck, they would always be as immune to disaster, always escape without a brain cell out of place. Richards, who had often feared for his sanity as a boy, battened strangely on his drug experiences, growing hugely in confidence and conviction; of what he was so convinced it was hard to say, but other people responded to him, they found his certainty attractive. Even Terry, in a covert way, took encouragement at Richards' source; the cool, distant brother-in-law, lone wolf though he might be, found sufficient reason to persist in his being, to stay the strange course he found implied by Richards' example. Then, when Richards' life suddenly fell apart — wife gone, job and prospects vanished in a trice; money all squandered, and even his dog, the ill-behaved Pomo, run off somewhere — it was as if an ancient, dire prediction had come freakily true, confirming Terry in his oldest, bleakest belief about the necessary downside of good times. In some ways, he took it even harder than Richards — though as Richards would later admit, in better form.

"She won't be coming back to you," his brother-in-law whispered one evening as Richards raved and blubbered in his empty house. "She's gone for good, man, because you treated her bad, *real* bad. And that's just the way it has to be."

The stark truth of these few words — and the need to comprehend them, to accept them — fairly took Richards' breath away. He could feel himself coming apart: his arms and legs actually seemed to detach themselves, his head to lift off.

"A woman is like a cat, man," Terry went on, "a sensitive, nervous cat. Once she's gone, she's really gone. You just can't get her back. On the other hand, a man's more like a dog — you can kick his ass, treat him like dirt, and he'll come back licking your hand. But Jackie's like a cat. She's always been that way — like a pretty, skittery cat. And now she's really gone."

For the immediate future, Richards was hardly in his right mind. He went begging after his vanished wife, whom he had alienated by his years of misbehavior. Terry's life coincidentally led away at that time, out of Richards' immediate orbit; their friendship, which had once seemed so important, so strangely promising, came to seem questionable, a mere artifact of the marriage, without an integrity or purpose of its own. When they ran into each other at the town tennis court, both seemed embarrassed yet also grimly pleased, as if the degree of their estrangement were cause for some perverse pride. If they, who had been scarily close, down in their souls, could now feel so little, then the universe was truly a ragged place, evilly amusing at best. They both wanted to laugh at it, rudely — just as the Mexicans, in one of Terry's letters home, had often laughed at badly crippled dogs.

"Hey — what's happening, man? What's new?"

"Nothing much. What *is* happening, is what I'd like to know . . ."

"Later, then."

"Yeah, well . . . later for that."

❧

In 1982, Richards spent a few weeks in Hawaii, mostly on the island of Oahu. As he came out of a Chinese restaurant one night, he saw Terry's old girlfriend Lonnie Samuels riding past in a convertible driven by an overweight brown-skinned man. Richards waved and called hello, but Lonnie neither waved nor looked his way.

Two nights later, he heard from her at his hotel. She had tracked him down by calling his brother, Joel, on Maui. Lonnie begged to be picked up at her apartment, where she was kept a virtual prisoner, at 11:45 that night; if Richards arrived any earlier, he might run into Tutua, her mad-dog boyfriend. Tutua and his brothers went out for drinks each weeknight at precisely 11:30. They usually returned after 1 A.M.

Richards performed as requested, and they made an escape in his rented Toyota, holing up not at his Honolulu hotel, where Tutua might sniff them out, but at a Motel 6 on the windward side. Lonnie had been living a nightmare of a familiar kind. Her part-Samoan, part-Ukrainian lover was jealous in the extreme, a violent person, cocaine user, collector of handguns, etc. Many times he had promised to do something "really bad" if he ever caught her so much as talking to another man; Richards suddenly felt that he had other places to be, better ways to be spending his vacation, but by then they were halfway to Kaneohe, and Lonnie was sobbing against his chest, hugging and kissing him in gratitude. Always an attractive girl, in a peasant-skirted, counterculturish way, she had metamorphosed into a true dishy beauty, a Honolulu nightclub fox. All those years of living out of a Volkswagen van had left no discernible mark, and she had entered the eighties with a vengeance. They stayed in Kaneohe for a week and a half. Lonnie had a cocaine propensity of her own, something modest, nothing out of the ordinary; and for want of something better to do, they made a little party of their situation. When the time seemed right Richards helped her close her bank accounts, collect a few belongings from friends, and prepare to leave the island for good. (Three years later he heard from her from Aspen, Colorado. She was living with an attorney, studying real estate management and meanwhile running a tanning salon.)

"You know," Lonnie said, toward the end of their days together, "I never really liked you, Richards. All those years of living at your house — I just thought you were so self-important, so selfish. It was always *your* house, *you* set the tone, though supposedly we were all one big happy family. I knew Jackie'd leave you in the end. I could see you both trying, really trying, but she was too good for you — too sweet, too true. And you were bored with her. You didn't want to be, but you were. I could tell."

Richards was taken aback by this sudden, categorical declaration. He admitted nothing, only cocked his head as if to hear better.

"Yeah, you wanted something different. Something larger and a little wilder, I guess . . . Have you found it yet, Richards, and is it any good? But you know, when I saw you that night, standing on the street outside of Bing Wong's, I got real excited. I knew I was saved, right then.

It's like what Terry used to say about you: 'Richards may be a jerk,' he'd say, 'he thinks he's King Shit, all right, but he usually comes through. You can count on him.' "

Richards absorbed this offhand, or seemingly offhand, confession for a long moment, in the end finding little that he wanted to argue with. Then he asked Lonnie what she had heard recently about her old boyfriend.

"Oh, it's pretty sad; he's just living on the street. Like a million other junkies, just hurrying up to die. Last I heard he was back in Darien. His father's dead now, and he asked his mother if he could stay in his old room. But she wouldn't have him. He's been stealing from her, you see . . . He and his brother broke in there, took her jewelry and stuff, a couple of summers ago. Real low-life junkie tricks."

Richards felt his heart twist up in his chest, and he grabbed her by the upper arm. He demanded to know how this could be: were they talking about the same man, about Terry, his ex-brother-in-law, her old boyfriend, their old housemate? Was it really Terry who had fallen this way, beautiful, good-for-nothing, wistful-cynical T.R., the same one who had shared Richards' life all those years? Who had been as close to him, from moment to moment, as any man had ever been?

"Yeah — who else? And let go of my arm, please, you're hurting me. You shouldn't act so surprised. He was always using, always. For a while there he hung in the balance, would he go this way, would he go that, but he wanted to be bad just a little bit more. Living in the mountains there, with you and Jackie to look after him, he could keep it together for a long time. It was just when you broke up and he had to go on his own that he fell apart."

Richards shook his head. He felt a kind of thrilling

coldness rising in him, a feeling so awful it was almost pleasurable, a torturing sort of chill that rushed up the backs of his thighs.

"I didn't know," he finally said. "I mean, I just didn't see. I had no idea. He never told me anything about it, and I never even guessed."

"No? You really didn't?"

"No. But I wasn't looking, either. And all that time I thought I was taking care of business — taking care of everybody's business. But I wasn't even awake."

" 'If you can remember the sixties,' " Lonnie quoted in a bright, winking tone of voice, " 'you weren't there.' Isn't that what they say?"

"Yeah, but I *was* there. I know I was. And now I'm starting to remember. I'm starting to remember everything."

RICHARDS REMEMBERED A COINAGE OF FRITZ Perls' from the sixties: "Guilt is unexpressed resentment." Just such a neat summation of things appealed to him once, not that he believed it, of course, not for a minute, but as an operating principle it had served. Yet now the sixties (and even their long-devolving aftermath, the seventies) were over, and he seemed to be reaping nothing but guilt, heaps of it. His ex-wife was lost to booze, cocaine, and a version of the lush life, and he blamed himself. Maybe she was happy being lost for a while, but he saw a tragedy. Meanwhile their daughter would never know a regular life, Mommy and Daddy in bed with each other, grumpy-content on a Sunday morning. Richards blamed himself.

His closest friends, at the dawn of the new decade, were experiencing psychic whiplash, massive disorders of the heart, divorcing, falling face down in the powder. Even here Richards felt partly responsible. In consequence of his belief in his own importance, he imagined that he had represented some sort of principle to them — call it the Jewish-Dionysian — and his arguments in favor of all manner of excess had urged them down dangerous paths. Now they hoped to enter the ordinary stream of life, but found they were ill suited — some, indeed, were virtually ruined. The sensitive pleasure nexus in each of us, designed to register the subtlest of stimuli, remembered caresses, opalescent dream shreds, had been blown apart. Orgasmic shocks on a steady basis had done it.

Richards no longer knew where he stood. Even on the question of The Orgasm itself, his old polestar and pal, he could no longer say of himself that he was somewhere to the right of Wilhelm Reich, to the left of Henry Miller, and suspended in the same bright, lewd ether as a Germaine Greer; yet neither had he turned his back on the thumping, shining cleave of heaven for good. He was indeed confused. Remorseful, too, and wanting to know the way: how to live so that he would never, ever hurt anyone again.

In May 1981 he received a dog-eared letter. Clearly it had followed his spoor over much hard terrain. An attorney in Sint Amandsberg, Belgium, wrote to ask if he was the same Abel Richards who had traveled in Europe as a college student fourteen years before. He was, and in that case a woman named Nicole Zwaff wished to be in contact with him. She wished him further to be aware of her son, Jean-Marc, now thirteen years old, who was without a doubt Richards' son.

The lawyerly letter struck fear, but there was an absence of demands, of evident entrapments. In the end, he was strangely moved to think that so tender, momentous a devoir had taken this frail form, that of a single sheet of onionskin sent over the seas to end up here, in his lonely mountain lair. He remembered Nicole Zwaff well, although her surname, in the days when he knew her, had been the less Flemish, more Gallicly evocative Soif. She was his first, most earthshaking grownup love. Seven years his senior, a poetess of many books, numinous beauty, mysterious presence, she had smiled upon him for some reason, and they had traveled around Spain in her Deux Chevaux. At the end of that landmark summer Richards' wisdom teeth were coming in. But he had needed to go back — he had to return to school. All along he'd lied to her about that, telling her he was older than he really was, already a "writer" of some kind.

Yes, it was possible. The math made sense. His first feeling was pride, joy, but then remorse took over, his new response to everything. A boy had grown up without a father, in a distant land, a bastard, practically a waif. Everywhere he had put his wand, it seemed, he made a hurtful magic. Several letters back and forth established a cordial, not particularly accusative tone between the woman and himself, and the photos she sent showed a sturdy, good-looking child, bespectacled, with the mother's fine, exotically slanted eyes precisely replicated. Soif had given way to Zwaff when she stopped publishing poetry, and for many years now she had been a professor of religion. She proposed a visit at Richards' convenience. Jean-Marc was eager to meet his father, she said.

Richards fretted. He punished himself both quietly and unquietly; of course he would go, maybe as soon as next year, but in what spirit, in what frame of mind? His love of those days, the even-tempered Rosemarie, advised him frankly against the trip, but seeing his growing intent she warned him to shrive himself first of every bit of guilt.

"If you go over there in this mood," she said, "asking to be forgiven, you'll make a bigger mess. The way I see it, an older woman picked up a handsome American college boy, had her way with him for a couple of months, and got a beautiful child into the bargain. You have nothing to apologize for. Don't think they need you to make their lives right, Richards — that's always been your problem, you exaggerate your own contribution. Other people make their own fates. You're not the central character in everybody's story."

"I know, Rose, of course I'm not. But the point of it is, I lied to her. I started out with lies, with subtle deceptions, and look what's come of it. I always lie to women. I'm not even conscious of it, most of the time . . . Lies of omission, but there you are. It's what I did with Jackie all those years ago. I should've sat her down at the beginning and said, 'I'm not good husband material, don't you see? I'm a raging satyr. Mad, bad, and dangerous to know. I'll break your heart someday, because I don't even know you're real.' "

Rosemarie didn't mind talking about Richards' ex-wife. She was imperturbable in many ways — on many subjects. "You're not a satyr, Richards, don't overreach. And if you were, just remember, there are nymphs among the women, too. Women have eyes in their heads, they know what they want. Maybe Jackie saw you for a bullshit artist from the very start. Maybe she even liked that about you. As for this other one, your fey poetess: I'd watch out. I think she knows what she wants, too."

Richards first heard his son's voice — deep, surprisingly manly — as he sneaked up the stairs in an apartment building in Destelbergen, a suburb of Gent. It was July of 1982. Nicole had left the door to her duplex open, and Richards heard the phrase "*Ach, moeder*" spoken in a tone of Flemish complaint. Such fondness was in this expression that he imagined he knew all there was to know, everything about this mother and son. He stood paralyzed at the front door, afraid to knock, sensing fateful things.

After a moment the boy wandered out of the kitchen, passing briefly through Richards' corridor of vision. He was dressed in short shorts, leather sandals with socks, and a wide-necked top with horizontal stripes such as Richards hadn't seen since his own boyhood, when mothers sometimes dressed their sons to look like little sailors. The brief sight of him gave Richards an odd, delicious feeling, as if the existence of some fabled beast, the snow tiger, the unicorn, had here been matter-of-factly confirmed. Seconds later Jean-Marc edged back into view. He, too, had seen something unaccountable.

"Oh. Please come in," he said, in unselfconscious English.

"I'm Abel Richards."

"Yes. I know who you are."

They shook hands.

"I'm sorry I'm a little late. The buses . . . I had a hard time finding the right tram, despite your mother's instructions."

Why was the boy smiling? He looked positively gleeful. Was it at Richards' description of himself as being "a little late," just a little bit?

"Please — come in. Mother prepares us a big breakfast. And now, it can be lunch."

Richards handed over some gifts. Nicole entered from the kitchen, wearing an apron, brushing her hair from her eyes; because her hands were dusted with flour, she could use only a little finger. Richards shrank back from her. Was this really the woman he had known — had he actually been a companion, an intimate, of this extraordinary beauty? And why was she so little changed after fifteen years? She looked at him with alert gravity, almost sternly, then seemed to find cause for amusement, possibly in his own baffled expression, possibly in the hopelessly overwrought situation. "Oh, Abel, you've finally come," she said. "At last, we can eat breakfast."

"It's so good to see you, Nicole. You look wonderful. Here, I've brought you something. Open it."

They didn't live as poorly as Richards had anticipated. The apartment was spacious, full of polished pine furniture, watercolors, and window light; it was welcoming and comfortably clean. He hadn't bothered to imagine the significance of Nicole's becoming a professor of religion, but now he noticed the profusion of crucifixes and other parochial signs, in particular a rugged cross mounted on top of a bookcase, a sturdy construction of tree limbs and fuzzy twine. Later he was to roam at will among her bookshelves, discovering how the poet of blood ceremonies, of Lorcaesque yearnings and Baudelairian tendencies, had metamorphosed into a scholar of Küng, Merton, and other religious thinkers whose names he didn't recognize. She had read exhaustively in contemporary as well as classical theology in French, Dutch, English, German, Greek, Latin, and Hebrew, and her own scholarly writings already filled half a shelf.

She taught at an institute in Gent, and several times in the last few years she had traveled to Israel, where the institute sponsored her in an ongoing research project. By the afternoon of the first day they were heatedly discussing the sorry state of Richards' Jewish soul: ardently philo-Semitic, knowledgeable in the way of an English major who yet astounds with her grasp of physics, she reproved him for his lack of observance, refusing to accept his customary excuse, that he was only "half" Jewish (but on the mother's side, which was all that mattered). A few days later, when they took Jean-Marc to see *Chariots of Fire,* she was much moved by the Ben Cross character, who suffers as a Jew at Cambridge. She asked Richards to tell them all about his own sufferings as a Jew in America. He had little to report.

He began to remember that summer, fifteen years before, when they traveled together: had there been signs of this religiosity even then, and had he ignored them or, more likely, taken them for signs of a delicious foreignness, an exotic Europeanness? They had visited many churches in their leisurely tour of Andalusia, Richards imagining himself to be Jake Barnes as they stood in the vaulted gloom of yet another nave, ". . . and I burnt a candle and prayed for all the things I want and won't ever get and we came out in a very fine mood," Nicole perhaps less ironic than he imagined in her devotions. Her spirituality, to give it its proper name, was a kind of pantheism, a finding of divinity in simple objects, in the natural mundane. The very foods they ate, the fields they hiked through, the tapestries, tilework, and Moorish murals they encountered in the towns, all touched her with an impossible keenness, imprinted upon her undefended soul. Richards, having never looked at things in quite this way before, felt the stirrings of change in himself. The burger-eating college boy, precocious skirt-chaser, avid collector of adventures and experiences (which he might brag on later), felt called to something finer.

There had been a kind of worship: an instinctive sort of

devotion. It was less a matter of churches, however, than of an intuitional aesthetic response, and Richards could hardly separate it from the other main element, the sex call, their prolonged, intense, slowly evolving mutual intoxication. They traveled for weeks before actually getting around to doing it, and never before had Richards experienced such a sustained, delicious spell, the outcome never for a moment in doubt, yet the moment waiting endlessly for its ripeness. When Nicole finally gave herself to him, she did so with a touching, offhand simplicity that completely unmanned him: how was he, so newly awakened to beauty and goodness, to act with such a prize? But act he had done. And she was deeply relieved, as he remembered. She could hardly thank him, praise him enough. He came to see that there had probably been few others before him; her beauty was of a rare type, flawless, complete unto itself. Certain eyes (he remembered thinking at the time), certain fine mouths, speaking words sweetly, define a quality that cannot be explained or finally construed; certain eyes, giving evidence of human thought and feeling, suggest a perfection without end, beauty outlasting the span of those who possess it.

Certain gestures, viewed at leisure in the vibrating shade *(la sombra temblorosa)* of some Andalusian orchard, "*donde viven los olivos centenarios,*" orchards of hundred-year-old olive trees, cannot be forgotten. Certain delirious, García Lorca–ish moods, maximally indulged, can give the movements of a woman's hands the weight of fatality. The affair lasted hardly a month. Yet Richards had not forgotten nor, in a way, had he ever stopped thinking of her. Now it struck him as incredible, outrageous, that her hands should still look the same, still fascinate with the slow, precise contouring of their indications (*"piensa que el mundo es chiquito, y el corazón es inmenso,"* she thinks the world is tiny and the heart immense). She was thinner than he remembered, not tall, physically quiet. The smell of her wrists was the smell of rosewater, blond wood, and fruit, powerfully reminiscent. "Ah," she said, when at last Richards was seated at her kitchen table, "now we eat. Now, at last, we can have our little meal."

❧

For several weeks he stayed on in Gent, traveling out from his hotel to see them each day, getting to know the boy. She had no car or telephone at her place, and he arrived each morning on a borrowed bicycle, after which they went to picnic somewhere. Jean-Marc, who asked to be called just plain Mark, like a real American boy, was a pleasure to know, direct, intelligent, hungry for fun. He was childish in his ability to wind whole romances around a single object, for example, the infielder's glove that Richards had improbably brought him; a chrome-plated fountain pen, with a tiny digital watch above the pocket clip, seemed to him the most cunning thing ever, exactly what you needed for those late nights writing letters, poems, or school reports.

A big reader of the funnies, he liked airplanes, cars, and corny practical jokes. He read the entire collection of Jack London stories Richards gave him, particularly relishing the goriest ones. His English was confident, resourceful. Nicole had been enriching his schoolboy fare for years in preparation for just this encounter, and in other ways as well she had gotten him ready to meet his father. Richards waited to be asked the hard questions, for example, why he had disappeared, why he hadn't married Nicole, who the hell he thought he was; but the boy was merciful. If they had time — if this was but the first of many such meetings, if they were really to know each other someday as father and son — there would be better moments.

On that score — whether they were actually father and son — Richards entertained not the slightest doubt. His first glimpse of Jean-Marc convinced him: they had the same sturdy, mesomorphic body, the same high-heeling way of walking, and on one of their picnics in the countryside, they both misplaced their spectacles after napping, then put each other's on. There was not a diopter of difference. That this spirited, handsome European child, with his pixie-ish haircut and scuffed bare knees, should have inherited the mark of Abraham, the ancient, Talmudic myopia, seemed to Richards both a stroke of ill luck and a wondrous bit of cosmic play.

At first diffident with each other, soon they were wrestling and grabbing at every opportunity. They went swimming at a men's club, and in the dressing room Richards suddenly understood the reason the boy had requested this outing: here it was, the primal scene, the son staring in some perplexity at the naked, storied member of the father, garnering such impressions as he could. And Richards stared back, encompassing the smooth, perfect body of his only son. Then they put on their bathing suits, engaged in wet horseplay.

Nicole was frankly joyful. This was all she had wanted, that the two of them should come to know each other, sense each other directly. She asked Richards' opinion on matters of discipline and schooling, and in the evenings she contrived for them all to be comfortable together, either in the city, where she knew interesting cafés and music halls, or in her apartment. An occasional smoker of an unfiltered cigarette, Richards found packs of Gauloises on the table next to the armchair he often occupied. Then there were many dinners, interesting people coming from all over western Belgium just to meet him; Nicole, still esteemed for the lurid poetry written in her youth, knew dozens of artistic types, *le tout Gent* as well as *le tout Bruxelles,* and she wished for them to meet her son's father, who happened to be an American writer. Often the guests included priests, scholars, and Catholic seekers of a dour aspect, who gathered about Nicole as about some figure of unquestioned spiritual distinction. The flavor of the discourse, as far as Richards could determine, was Teilhard de Chardin–ish, with talk of "omega points," "radial energy," and of course, the inevitable Parousia.

Every night, after dining well and playing Ping-Pong with Jean-Marc, having smoked his cigarette in the courtyard garden, Richards would bike meditatively back into the gray city, to his room at a railroad station hotel. Nicole offered him the living room couch one night, after a gathering lasted till one in the morning, but Richards said no: he was paying for his room in any case, so he might as well go back.

They found a few minutes to be alone, to talk about the past. Richards had prepared an extensive mea culpa, but Nicole hardly wanted to hear: she had forgiven him as one forgives a friend's faux pas, something it's best not to talk about anymore.

"You were young, Abel, that's all. We were both very

young, selfish. Too hungry for life, I think. But is that wrong? Isn't it right to be warm to life — to welcome it, to want to seduce it? Take life for a powerful lover, because we only have this one moment, I think. Don't you agree?"

They had drunk half a bottle of wine together, and her coloring slowly deepened. Richards stared at her throat as if at something unaccountable, the silken stretch of lucent skin slowly enrouging, taking on the very tint of the Pomerol.

"I don't know, Nicole. Sometimes I'm not sure I even have this moment, it keeps slipping away from me . . . When I think of how I behaved then, how greedy I was, just for sensations, because sensations were never satisfying to me, never quite enough . . . well, I'm ashamed. I came on with such urgency all the time, without really knowing what I wanted. Other people just got swept along . . . and I had this weird, hammering sort of need in my head all the time. More of an intellectual thing than anything else. Here — have a little more wine."

Her smile was knowing; she accepted the merest splash of the Bordeaux. Just that evening, she'd entertained a circle of her graduate students, most of them young women, who had all but kneeled at her feet. They had asked simple/profound questions, as for instance, "I feel called, Mlle. Zwaff, but I know how flawed I am — how painted with sin. I distrust my feelings for good reason. So, what should I do?" Another had talked about her mother's terminal cancer as "a beautiful gift, the most precious tie between us, because it brings her closer to *Him,* may He have mercy on her in these last days." Richards had never seen faces quite like these before, this kind of luminous, questing solemnity. On hearing that he was a writer of novels and film scripts, they turned away in sadness and distaste. Nicole smiled knowingly at that, too.

The sheer improbability of their connection impressed itself upon him: how had this Virginal Mother, this sanctified flower of Flanders, come to intercept his life trajectory with her own, to add her purity, idealism, and earnestness to his demotic surge? How had she arrived at that place and time, in that receptive frame of mind, that allowed them to begin together at all? She had given herself, as he remembered, as one gives a precious, singular gift, which was the only way to go, he had come to believe, after so many heedless years; yet given herself to just the wrong sort of man (or boy), to one who wanted only to spend himself, to make nonchalant, reckless gestures in the face of fate. Their pairing was fundamentally incongruous — senseless in a way.

"You know," she said to him one evening, "I think we are actually much alike. You write your books, and I do the same. Each night you sit in the chair and read your French novel, with the *Larousse* at your side, because you're in Europe now, and you think you must do something serious. But this is what I do every day. Read texts, always the old texts. And you have a lonely life, I think, despite maybe many women. Devoted to your young child, to your little Margaret. Just as I live only because of Jean-Marc."

"Nicole," he said, "I don't understand why you've never married. You're the most beautiful woman I know. No, don't be embarrassed, listen to me . . . You'd like to have a man, you like the whole idea of it. I can tell you do."

"Of course I like men, Abel. And I have had some good ones, who wanted me in a real, authentic way. But now let me tell *you* something. This will embarrass *you,* I think . . .

that there are only a few people sometimes, only one or two in a life. And if you care about the feeling you have with the one, then you don't marry so easily. Maybe you never marry at all."

Richards considered this statement for a long moment, finally deciding not to take it altogether personally. "All right — very well. But why do you dishonor the feeling, the unique feeling, if you then go out and find someone else? Don't you have a responsibility to try to be happy? To make a decent life if you possibly can? And you'll still have the other always, because you remember it. Maybe it just wasn't meant to be lived."

After a moment she replied, "No. I cannot agree." Her pale eyes, gathering the low lamplight, inflicted a kind of reproving intensity upon him. "I don't think you believe that, either. You haven't married so often, I happen to notice. And I know who you are, remember. Maybe it was long ago, but I knew you quite well. I understood you, just as you understood me."

"Did I? Really?"

"Yes, you read my poems. That crazy, fatally romantic girl I was, the one who was always about to scream inside . . . Well, that's who I am, even now. Still the same."

As he readied himself to leave at midnight, Nicole came against him, then turned her lips up quickly, just barely touching his own. It was more of a breath than a kiss, yet the flavor of it marked him — it stayed with him for hours.

He wondered what they were getting up to, and he began to look at her differently, relaxing somewhat his stiffness and correctness. Maybe it was less necessary than he thought that he exude this regretfulness, this tentative rue, which had been his way of paying her a kind of respect. A small woman, rather severe in dress, whose hands and eyes effortlessly captivated, she created a perverse effect with her nunnish manners and now, since their evening of the too-much Pomerol, her occasional suggestive looks and tones of voice. Once in the kitchen, with seven people seated at the table in the other room, she rearranged the pastries on the tray that Richards was to carry out for her, pressing her hand against the small of his back and her pelvis against his hip, causing so specific and lustrous a feeling that he almost stopped breathing. It was as if some perfect master, some tantric adept, had contacted his very center with a thought.

"Nicole — what are you doing?"

"Well, as you see, Abel. As you see."

"Yes, but what are you thinking of when you do that? What's on your mind?"

"Please — don't be boring. And take that out now."

Usually she was not coquettish, for which he was grateful; it was more of a fatally romantic, a romantically fated, feeling she evinced, to which Richards found himself extraordinarily responsive. All those years before, traipsing through the south of Spain together, camping near the Alhambra or sleeping, pretty chastely, in an old hotel on the bay in Málaga, all bougainvillaea and orange trees, they had conjured this same feeling, subsisted on it as upon some divine bread. She had a gift for love, whereby all her words, all her movements and expressions, became symbols of it. Her being existed in a different space-time continuum, and Richards sometimes looked about nervously at the other dinner guests, or at the patrons at the nearby tables in Le

Moulin à Poivre, a café they often visited, to see if they had caught the fractional slowing down of time, the slight thickening and darkening of the atmosphere around her hands, as she passed him a piece of cake. As far as he could tell, they had not. Along with her aptitude for endless suggestion, for symbol making, she had the cognate gift of postponement, as if seduction must be a long, complex act, infinitely and deliciously prolonged. In the best of all possible worlds, it would never actually transpire, only approach endlessly; the play leading up to it could not, however, be said to be therefore any less ecstatic, any less fulfilled.

She moved him with her strong need, and he marveled at this love capacity, this rare romantic soul, which was buried within her and in some ways denied by her responsible, spiritual aspect. On their picnics with the boy she often sat apart, her skirts spread demurely on the grass, reading, yet Richards was as keenly aware of her as if she had sat there naked, with her throbbing heart exposed in her breast. She had touched him once, in the kitchen, kissed him only that single time as he biked off in the darkness; but he was hers. The insane idea of recapitulating their affair, dredging up the old feelings, possibly even reenacting the abandonment — mutual or not, it had been mostly his own work, he came to feel, largely his own fault — seemed quite reasonable, and he awaited developments passively.

"You know, Abel," she said to him once, "I'm an old woman now. I'm already forty-two. I can't have children anymore, because I've had an operation. My breasts are a mother's breasts. I often feel tired, and I think I won't live much longer — maybe only another few years."

"But why do you say such a thing, Nicole?"

"I've made a mistake in my life, I know. Some great error that came from pride, from my pure mind power, believing I was better than other people. And I was always afraid of being a real woman. But I can't live any other way. I must commit this error, over and over. And seek God. That's all I know in life."

He saw her differently: as a thoughtful, generous woman, an inspiration to her many students, a loving and dependable mother, a resourceful friend. She was only a little pious sometimes — that was all he could think to hold against her.

"Why do you say you're afraid to be a woman? Everything you do is so womanly, Nicole . . . how you greet people, even how you touch things. We're not allowed to say this in America anymore, but there's a magical quality to what a real woman does, an openhearted, womanly woman . . . You have that quality, maybe more than anybody I've ever known. And don't talk about living only a few years. It's bad luck."

He asked to see her books of poetry, as they were not displayed on her shelves. She produced a carton containing many publications, some in French, some in Flemish. After a while she drew his attention to a slender volume entitled *Tango Mortale*. It was written in Flemish, and the young poetess was depicted on the cover, posed in a meadow beside a pygmy goat.

"This one," she said, "is a book about a wild, roguish lover I had. I pray he never reads it. Although, as I recall, once that's all I hoped: that he would read it, read it and suffer. It's a bad, hateful book, full of hard thoughts. It made people be afraid for me."

"May I have this? May I keep this copy?"

"No. I don't think so. You can't read the Flemish, anyway."

"Well, I'll have Jean-Marc translate for me."

She became very alert. "You must never do that, Abel. No — please, promise me. I'm quite serious about it."

"Well, I don't know if I *will* promise . . ."

She picked up the books, took them quickly out of the room.

One day she arranged a short trip. They borrowed a neighbor's car, packed bathing suits and food, and aimed for the North Sea. Richards had begun to feel lethargic, as often happened when he waited for some important development in his life, and he was afraid to drive the car, thinking he might fall asleep at the wheel. The day was soft and wonderfully fragrant in the grassy fields. Before they reached the shore he felt as if they were driving through an enormous flower, one whose contours could only be apprehended through all the senses at once, sight and smell but also a new sense having much to do with this dreaminess he felt, this blissful lack of will. At the ocean, Jean-Marc frolicked with the young friend they'd brought along, and Richards changed reluctantly into his bathing suit, then made himself stand for a moment in the gray surf. It was murderously cold, but even this didn't wake him up. Nicole also changed her clothes, also waded out. She took Richards by the hand, looked seriously up into his face.

"Don't be troubled, Abel. We haven't done anything wrong, so far. Oh, I'm just so happy to see you again. Yes, there is something, it happens again. But that's all. I'm happy just to feel it again."

"Nicole, I want to think about things this time. I want to act well with you. But I feel overwhelmed. I'm absurdly comfortable with you, I can't gather my thoughts. They're somewhere out there, out in the gray ocean. I know how atypical this is, just like our trip in Spain, happening outside of time. You know that, too, I think. But it doesn't seem to bother you. Look at you — there's a pearly, salty dust on your mouth. Here, and on your cheek."

He kissed her then, a real kiss, and felt that he understood his passivity now, that it was a refusal not to speak this way, not to make love to her with words; not to be this absurd lover-figure whom he impersonated so easily. It would have taken real will not to. They were standing among the other bathers, among the picnic hampers, the changing booths, the crazily colored towels. Nicole turned away from him, looking for Jean-Marc and the other boy. Still in the sea. A woman on a nearby hillock, a fleshy person wearing a yellow swimsuit with green stripes, gazed at Richards as if at a curious tree, a mere feature of the landscape, something without an answering consciousness. He noticed that her right foot was loosely bandaged.

"Nicole, of course I want you," he said. "But I can't be something important for you. I know that about myself now. I don't mean I don't feel something wonderful when we touch, for example, something absolutely real. But I only go this far. This fantasy we have, it's just too strong . . . this family we could already be, you and me and the boy. It's just too strong. I don't know what to do about that. Or about you — because you move me, you break my heart."

After a moment she replied, "But what is that supposed to mean, Abel? How do I break your heart? I haven't done anything to hurt you, as far as I know. And please, don't kiss me, then start to pity me, even before I can catch my breath. It isn't *gentil.*"

"I'm sorry. That isn't what I meant at all."

The boys came out of the sea. The friend of Jean-Marc's was a tall, heavyset boy with a ruddy face. He was holding his right hip and crying; he had been stung by something in the deep water. The boys came up the beach quickly, Jean-Marc a few steps in the lead, unaware that his friend, just behind, was clutching his side and grimacing. Richards and Nicole walked down to meet them.

"What is it, Luc?" she asked, touching his side with her pale hand. "What hurts you there?"

He blubbered something to her in Flemish. There was an angry welt just above his hip, a line seven or eight inches long, as straight as if it had been drawn with a ruler. Jellyfish came into the sea here sometimes, she explained, though this was not the season. She hadn't thought to be on guard.

"I know," she said soothingly. "It hurts terribly." She held him in her arms. "Come, Luc. Come. I have some cream in my bag, I think."

The boy only stood, sobbing. He dipped his head meekly against her neck. She waited patiently.

"Come with me, Luc. We'll find you something."

As they gathered up their belongings — Nicole and the boy had hurried up the beach, seeking a lifeguard — Richards and Jean-Marc exchanged glances. Richards could see that his son was upset, despite or perhaps because of fierce attempts not to burst out laughing. Then the woman in the yellow bathing suit, the one who had stared at Richards, approached and began to speak to them in idiomatic Flemish, followed by a few phrases of rapid and idiomatic

French. Finally he began to understand as she pointed urgently to her bandaged foot: she, too, had had an accident, had also been stung out of season.

He left for Paris, where some friends were expecting him on the fifteenth of August. As he emerged from the metro stop at Odéon and beheld the facades of the Place Henri-Mondor, as he wandered in dismay along the Boulevard St.-Germain, he was stricken as if with a fatal virus, and a sensation such as he had only read about in books overwhelmed him. But he had never really lived in Paris, only passed leisurely through that summer fifteen years earlier. How had this city then become the very talisman of his loss, symbol of the hunger of his hopeful youth? These sycamores and chestnut trees, standing in the foreign air of Paris, moved him maddeningly — they had remained, and in their branches still tangled shreds of his boyish self, which had once walked beneath them. The hotel at which he'd stayed for two weeks that summer, an undistinguished edifice off the Rue St.-Jacques, looking now much brighter, more spruce than he recalled (Chirac had recently scrubbed Paris), loomed at a turning of the boulevard. Standing on the street corner, looking up at the ironwork balconies, he felt that he must surely be losing his mind.

He was afraid of so much feeling: of not knowing what to do with it, of having no way to evade it. Loss was all he could think of, all he could feel. For three days he looked for himself in the streets, finding the forms of old friends and lovers. At the church of St.-Étienne du Mont, where once he had picked up a French-Swiss girl, lovely, gray-eyed, a night or two in another hotel, he sat on a wooden pew and quietly wept. An old Frenchwoman, clad in black, walked past and briefly squeezed his shoulder.

But what did he really want — for what did he yearn? Surely his youth was gone, he had squandered himself in just such follies as his thoughtless, too numerous amours; yet would he be happier not to have had them? That quality of breathless, keen expectation of youth, that feeling of life encountered with whole curiosity, the future to be conjured, was lost to him, but so what? It happens to all. We all lose that, in fact, it may be the easiest of the later losses, and he had never much cared before. But he had really lived here: that summer rich in consequences, consciously, vividly lived, remained here in some ghostly form, still haunted the boulevards. At moments he felt that he could almost recover it.

His good friends, world travelers now at the end of a year-long circumnavigation, were established at the Hotel Crillon. They received him with gifts, champagne, expressions of concern. The wife said he looked haunted. The husband, Richards' best college friend, had experienced an awakening on a remote Indonesian island, and he clothed himself now in Balinese fabrics, even at the Crillon. He was tired; he had seen too much, traveled too far, he said. He was returning to the States with a feeling of vast relief.

"I wrote to the medical school again," he explained. "On the one hand, I'm thirty-six now, but on the other, I'm not yet thirty-seven. It isn't all over for me, is it? And if they won't take me, then I'll apply to school in Mexico. I know what I want to do."

The wife explained, in a voice drained of her customary irony, that her husband had roamed the island of Taliabu for several days, eating nothing but the acorn-shaped psilocybin mushrooms abounding there. Eventually he had a sort of vision, in which he came to understand that he might one day be a healer, an easer of human suffering. In the end he saw no reason not to honor this idea.

"It's a little strange, but I feel good about it. I have some hope, for the first time in years."

"I think it's wonderful, Eric," Richards said promptly. "Who cares where the ideas come from, just so they come? And you can handle all my medical work from now on. For free, of course."

The wife, Saskia, remembered why Richards had come to Europe in the first place. He found that he had much to say about his visit with his unknown son, but a strange unwillingness to speak out loud: it was too soon to commit to his feelings, to own his sensations.

"The boy is just wonderful," he said, "and they were very kind to me. They took me everywhere, introduced me to everybody. I met the old grandmother who lives out in Ypres, where they had the bloodiest battles of World War I. Monstrous, god-awful slaughters, and each spring she turns up bones in her garden. Hundreds of human bones."

"But what about the mother, Richards?" Saskia insisted. "Tell us about the woman. That's what I want to know about, of course."

"She was very welcoming, as I said. In some ways, she's different from the person I knew before, but in other ways not too much. She's a full professor now. She writes books on Catholic doctrine, things like that. Each day she rides her bike to the institute, and her students there adore her. They're more like disciples than students."

"Oh, I see," said the wife after a pause, with a return of

irony. "The life of sin now to be expiated. Get thee behind me, and all that. But how was she toward *you,* Richards — what did she make of you?"

"I don't know. We only talked a few times . . ."

She became disturbed, thinking he was hiding something from her, and for the next two days she probed relentlessly, because she could tell that something had happened to him. But Richards could not be made to speak freely, and when he left his infection immediately returned, his virulent nostalgia, and he felt half-mad with hopelessness. Yet he was not, in any objective sense, without hope. He was still the same man he had been before, still someone with a life back in California, a beloved daughter, prospects. The feeling of desolated, bottomless regret could not last, he told himself; it was only a summation of all he had been feeling, a culmination of the insane remorse of the last few years. On the train back into Belgium, his indulgence of this feeling lessened, and he began to relax. He had only needed to put some miles between himself and the reminiscent force-field that was Paris: that had been his only problem, he saw.

He would return to Gent, there to see his son again briefly, and Nicole. The boy had gone off camping while Richards went to France. Then in four more days he had his flight back to California. He was looking forward to it.

As the train crossed the border a woman knocked on the door of his compartment. She had been sitting elsewhere, but a man there was smoking cigars, and she asked if she could come in. Richards said yes, of course.

She was only twenty, a university student recently arrived from Senegal. As she had no English, they made their way in Richards' troubled French, with uncertain results.

Soon they got on to the subject of Paris. She had seen Paris for the first time only this past month, and she was overwhelmed: nothing in her life had prepared her for it, for the spectacle of it, the enchantment.

"My father spoke of Paris, because he himself was a student there, thirty years ago . . . Still, I had a completely false idea. There can be no experience through another person, don't you agree? When I arrived I felt strange, almost sick, and I found a room where I could be by myself. I stayed in this room for sixteen days. I only came out because the people from the embassy found me . . . If they hadn't thought to look, I would still be there, still terrified." She laughed aloud, and Richards, a little startled, also began to smile.

"I had so many ideas, you know. Political ideas, ideas about anticolonialism, which are good ideas, of course . . . But you know, sometimes a river just takes you by the throat, when you have only waded in, thinking just to clean your feet. It was like that for me. I come from Dakar, too, from a large, beautiful African city. I am not a simple village girl, you know. I have been to the university two years. After staying at the embassy a few nights, I vanished into the city, into magical Paris, and they have never found me since. Now I'll go on to Amsterdam. I wish to study biochemistry there."

Richards listened to her adventures, which were the experiences of a warm, questing girl from another world, someone who had attracted notice and kindness. He was puzzled and disbelieving, thinking that of all the people who might have tapped at his compartment door, it was she, another searching youth, a dark, cross-sexual doppelgänger of his, who, while he had been roaming the rueful boulevards, had been having the time of her life. Something she said made him suspect that there had been a love affair, too, a delicious little fling, and he credited this influence with her extraordinary forthcomingness now, her need to confess to the likes of him, a pale, worried-looking stranger, someone who kept resting his forehead in his hands.

"But monsieur — are you well?" she finally asked. "I must be boring you. It's only because you said that you had just been to Paris — and that you love Paris. I can't stop thinking about it. I think that I must always remember it now."

After a long moment he replied, "No, I'm not bored — not at all. On the contrary, I'm so moved by what you say. When I was your age I had some experiences, Parisian experiences . . . What I can't understand is why it makes me so sad now, as if I had lost everything there. You only hope for a little while this way, only once or twice in your life. When you find that life begins to yield to you, accepts your dreams, that's the great discovery, I think. The one really wonderful thing. Go on, now, go back to Paris. Don't go on to Amsterdam — what for? The way you felt in Paris is the way you ought to feel. You looked so happy, telling me about it. I could tell how hopeful you are."

He felt choked, full of emotion and ludicrous self-awareness; these windy sentiments he was expressing, they were all he could summon, no matter how earnestly he tried. Yet their very banality moved him. There was a gap he could probably never bridge between what he felt and what he had the courage to say; and this was a human failing, something he could probably forgive in himself.

"Go on," he continued, "go back to Paris. Things will

happen for you there. Have you got some money? Well then, by all means, do it . . . The point is to act, act while you still have that hope. Later on it isn't so easy. You come to know yourself too well. You can't do what you want, even when you try to, when other people need you to. You only have this opportunity for a short while. It's all because of that hope you feel."

The young student looked at him gravely — her expression bespoke perplexity as well as a kind of fear. "But you see, monsieur, everything is already arranged. I have matriculated already at the university. I have studied Dutch already, for two years. It isn't a question of living in Paris — that's simply not possible for me. The facilities are inferior, in the first place. And in the second, I *want* to go to Amsterdam, I sincerely want to . . ."

They spoke for another few minutes, the train seeming to fall, to collapse continually forward through the rhythmic night. Richards realized that he was very tired. Finally he slept. Just before Gent, the young woman woke him and explained where they were.

There was an opportunity to speak, but finally there was no need. Nicole looked at him closely as he walked through her apartment door, then smiled briefly. She showed him where to put his suitcase.

"You may stay here tonight, Abel, if you like. Tomorrow, you can return to your hotel."

"Thank you. I'd like to stay here tonight."

While in Paris he had bought more gifts, and he presented these when Jean-Marc came home. For the boy an assortment of classic, stupid props (disappearing coin box, vomit mat, squirting pinky ring), and for the mother, a scarf of luminous silk. She pulled the scarf from its box and tented it with her long fingers, and it became exquisite, alive. She looked Richards in the eye, in her almost-stern way, and thanked him.

"It's Italian," he said. "As soon as I saw it I thought of you."

"Yes, these are colors I used to wear. And now I will again, for a while longer."

While wandering in the Marais he had found a shop of a peculiar type, one that sold nothing but marionettes, hand puppets, and related paraphernalia. He bought four hand puppets to give to his daughter, Margaret, who would expect a substantial gift when he returned from his lengthy travels.

"Two plaster princesses," he explained, "one blond, one brunette. Very beautifully painted. Here — let me show you." He unpacked the puppets for inspection. There were two wooden ones as well, a bearded king and a stalwart young soldier.

"Your sister," he advised Jean-Marc, "is a lot like you. She always plays hard, can't get enough fun. She wears everything out in just a couple of weeks. Nicole once described you to me as 'a cross between a bulldozer and a philosopher,' something like that. Isn't that true, Nicole? And Margaret's a lot like you. Of course, she's only a little girl. We don't know how much she'll philosophize yet."

"I think that my sister must be a good child," Jean-Marc replied solemnly. "And I like what you tell me about her. Maybe she's a little curious, thinking that she has a brother so far away. Someone bigger than she is, who would protect her."

They ate a good meal, Richards providing a red Burgundy of some reputation. As he took a bite of lemon tart the plate on which it sat began to rise and fall, as if the tabletop were pulsing, and the boy broke into cackles, exposing the rubber bulb he had placed under Richards' mat. He could cause the plate to move by squeezing another bulb in his lap.

"A rubber vein runs from here," he said, a thin tube concealed beneath the tablecloth. Richards marveled at this clever device and its emplacement.

"Now you've played a good trick on me," he admitted. "But I'll have to get even. It could happen at any time. Tonight, tomorrow, maybe next year. You'll never know."

"Oh, Father. No, don't say that . . ."

The boy went happily to bed, and Richards thought about going down to the courtyard for a smoke. He felt that Nicole expected him to, and so he went. She was sitting at her desk when he returned, reading a manuscript. He sat in the blue armchair. An hour later she stood up, collected the pages in a box, and announced that she was going to bed.

"Sleep here if you like," she said. "But if you prefer, come upstairs. That would please me, I think."

"Nicole?"

She had turned away. She looked back briefly.

"Turn out the lights," she instructed, "but leave this one on. Don't bother to shutter the windows. It's a warm night. Let the air flow through."

"Nicole, I want to be with you, very much. But first let's say what this doesn't mean. Let's be honest with each other. I want to speak the truth."

"Oh, Abel. Once you were so wise. When you were

only twenty years old, you knew just what not to say to a woman . . . and now you've forgotten everything. What has happened to you? I don't care what this doesn't mean. I don't even care about what it does mean, if anything."

He had been wanting her, but when he lay beside her he was frightened by the sudden chaos of his feelings, a vast, spinning disorder that seemed to surround them in her narrow bed. He felt for a while as if he were back on that Paris train, falling continually forward through the dark. Her room was a monk's cell, Spartan and severe, softened only by her rosy scent. For several minutes he simply lay there, hoping to calm himself. She took off her blouse and her brassiere.

"Abel, I can't even hear you breathe," she finally complained. "Are you still here? Are you alive?"

"I'm remembering, Nicole. Just remembering. Thinking about everything."

"Oh, please — don't remember me, Abel. Try not to. Instead, put your hand here. Feel how old I've become. That's what I am now. That's who I really am."

"I know who you are, Nicole. And I want you, with all my heart. Maybe too much. It's just like before."

The words came from within him, they were truthful in a way, he thought; but they were only a lover's easy words. But it was all right, even so. He knew how to do this — how to touch her, how to speak love to her. Their clothes burned off their bodies. He became quickly aroused, thinking of everything, of his body with hers, of this mutual act, which seemed somehow the right thing to do. He felt thankful to have this way to be with her.

She made a few sounds, not in any of her languages. He found her to be very soft and precious, fragrant and changing. At one point he heard a fierce, profound intake of breath, followed by as profound an exhalation. The whole point seemed to have been that moment, her arriving at a single instant of free breathing. He went on and on with her.

Later, he asked if Jean-Marc would care, finding them in the same bed together in the morning. She replied that he was fairly innocent for a boy of fourteen — not like some American children at all.

"If he does see us, he will understand in some way. I think he even wants that. Once in his life, to see his mother and father in bed together. It may be good for him."

"Nicole, I thank you for this. I thank you. Your beauty moves me, it makes me less afraid. It makes me think less of time. I'm happy that there's still this feeling between us — now I see it wasn't an accident all those years ago, it wasn't just something I forced to happen. And I still feel it. I feel all of it in my heart."

She smiled. "You are only a lover for me, Abel — that's all you want to be. But even so, I feel well now. I'm glad that you want to make love to me still. But it's a different feeling from those years ago. It's an odd, final type of feeling. Like something at the end of your life, uncompleted and sweetly bitter. It goes on, and I know I won't be able to understand it. I don't have enough time."

He kissed her. "You're wrong about that, I know you are. This gives you more time, don't you see? Making love makes more time. It's a little victory over time. But come on — I want you to help me now. I want us to do it all over again."

June 1990

Wednesday, 8:30 o'clock

DEAR FATHER,

It's been two months since my latest letter for you left this desk . . . so I guess it was some kind of priority now to make a new one.

First of all, I want to wish you great luck and happiness for your birthday. I'll also wish you a very good health (although I do believe that 43 is a little early to start making reservations in an old people's home — around 40 is rather just beneath the peak of "male strength" I think, anyway, I do wish you to be well).

When you arrive on the 2nd of July, I will be just finished with my first exam in maths. I think it was the right decision because I love it and I have a feeling of getting everything just right, everything in its just place, when I study maths or physics instead of something like language. I don't know what has happened to me, but the "dreamy kid" in me has finally gone away, and now I definitely want to pass my exams and move forward and think of getting a diploma. Funny how these things change, because only two years ago I didn't want to study and I have had many problems with my mother, as you know, for not going to the university, but now I put myself under such a pressure to succeed that I can almost not stand it! My exams will be until July 10 and my hardest are at the end, I think Analysis will be hardest. Yet my teachers say I have a kind of a little "gift" for understanding concepts, and I shouldn't think already just to be an engineer, but maybe a physicist. I don't know.

Let's turn to your trip now, that you're going to start in exactly one month. I will be at Brussels airport on Monday, 2nd of July, around 8:10 A.M., looking for a backpacked mountain climber sort of man, who looks a lot like me but is not taller anymore (!). I thought we might come to Gent then, and we could arrange our vacations for the next month. While I am struggling taking exams, you will be climbing the Weïsshorn, the Bishorn, the Obergabelhorn, and maybe some other horns I don't know about. But please be careful. All right, I know it isn't the place for the son to say to the father, Carry your umbrella in case it rains, but think what has happened. We have had some very bad luck. And I need my father now to talk to about some things, you know.

Thursday, 2:31 o'clock

Sorry, somebody came and things happened and I had to drop off writing this letter. But now I return and I promise to put it in the post tomorrow morning, first thing. (I mean, *this* morning!)

After you arrive, I will be completing my exams, and when you come back from Switzerland I'll be ready for some holidays. Now listen to my idea. Instead of coming to Gent to meet me, why don't you get on one of those perfect Swiss trains and go across the border into Germany, and I will meet you in Mainz, an interesting city, where I know two girls who have been studying in Gent sometimes. We'll stay in their father's hotel. (Don't worry, this is all arranged. One of the girls is not my girlfriend, but something like that, anyway.) Then I propose we get in my diesel Rabbit and drive around Germany, to Tübingen and to Heidelberg, where I went one time with my mother, when I was thinking to study Psychology, and to the Boden See on the Swiss border again, where there is excellent swimming. I know you have some funny feelings about Germany, as you wrote me two years ago, being a Jew from your mother. But I promise, I will protect you! I have an excellent German they say, much better than this rotten English, and I will be a good guide for you. In Tübingen, I stayed with my mother in a large tent, in a big camping on the bank of the Neckar river. I can find it again probably. I have saved my mother's tent and also her cooking stove, and some sleeping mats, and other things that we need to make a successful camping.

You know, the day when my mother was injured, they called me first from the hospital, but then I had to call my uncle and my grandmother, to tell them to come. Then I wanted to call you in America, because I felt something, that was like my mother speaking to me, telling me to call you now. I am so sorry I did not call you. There is nothing you could do, of course, but I believe she was really speaking, and two other times after I heard her speak again to me. It was just that first time, I wasn't ready to believe in this yet. And when I did call you it was already over.

As you know, she was sick for a long time, because of her spine that was growing with arthritis. She had to go to work every day in the city, but she always rode her bicycle because it felt good for her back, even though the doctors said it was right to be in a wheelchair by now. When she rode her bike, she looked very small and beautiful on it, wearing a dark raincoat usually and a scarf on her neck, and the day when she was hit by the car she was wearing a blue and silver cloth that you gave her for a present many years ago, that you bought in Paris. When she died after twenty-nine days in the hospital, they gave me this raincoat and this scarf.

I think she was ready to die. All the poems that I collected were about dying, that she wrote for the last two years and more. Maybe someday this will be her last book, if I find somebody to help me make it. When she was in the hospital, where her pelvis was broken and one of her lungs was also crushed, and her leg, and they expected her to die from bleeding inside, she woke up after a week there, and I think she was happy that she hadn't died. She was in pain, but she was happy not to die, I think. Then she started getting better, and I came to visit her every two days, on the average. We still argued about the university. I hadn't been such a good son, and I hadn't been going to visit her before she had to go to the hospital, so maybe it was a good thing, even though it was a terrible thing, because it made me go see her. If I had not gone every two days I think I would not be able to live, myself, now.

Then she got ready to go home, she was even putting on a stocking, on the leg that wasn't broken, and at that very moment her heart stopped. It was an embolism of the blood. The doctor said it was waiting for her, it would have happened. It was like her Fate.

I'm sorry — this all just comes out of me now. I don't mean to write it to you, you already know it, but here it is in my letter. I'm sorry that she didn't say anything about you when she was sick in the hospital, but I think she was thinking about you, because I read some of her last poems, the very last. When you come in July I want to ask you some questions about her. She never told me about when she met you, how that happened, except that you were too young for her, and you were still a student when you met. She said you were very handsome then.

Well, now — it's getting late. I'm not even sure what I'm writing to you anymore. I must go to sleep now, Father. I wish you a safe plane ride, and many thanks that you're coming. It's a good thing you do for me now, to come. We will have a good vacation. I want to talk to you. I hope to see you.

Your son in Europe,
Jean-Marc
whose sleepy eyes are
closing now, it's 4:10
o'clock in the morning

Sept. 4, 1990

DEAR JEAN-MARC,

All during my plane ride home, I was thinking of you, remembering all we talked about, and all we did not. I enjoyed our time together very much. It was very important to me. I feel I have a son now, and I hope you'll feel that you have a father, someone who loves you, who only regrets that he hasn't known you well till now, who wants to be known by you. All my life I've struggled against a certain feeling of not being real — not quite, not quite — but in what I feel for you I come into that happy zone. As you see, I'm being selfish even now; as you said one night, we Americans will work on our self-realizations right into the very deathbed, and maybe a little beyond.

But I think there's something you'll always hate me for, now that Nicole is gone. If she were still alive, if we could all have been together this summer, there might have been a reckoning, an answer to all of it (although I think not the answer she always wanted). But she isn't alive, and even for me — who, as you said, doesn't "need" to feel sad, meaning, I think, that I don't deserve to — there is a loss. A bitter loss. One whose shape I can't describe to you, and that I don't ask you to respect, but that I ask you to consider for a moment. Think of it as something small, undeserved, even ignoble; but do think of it.

What I'm concerned about is that this will always lie between us. I know that it has to, and it's probably right that it does, but I'm sending you these few pages anyway, not to excuse myself (they'll only damn me further) and not even to explain myself, but to give you a sense of what it was like for me all those years ago. At the time when I met your mother I was younger than you are now — again, not that this excuses me. But falling in love with her was the most signal experience of my life, and this summer, as you and I traveled in the Dauphiné and other areas that seemed familiar to me, I remembered all of it, I was actually sick with it, half-delirious with memory, and so I began to write this journal, which I now give you. It talks about the summer twenty-three years ago when I met your mother, what happened between us, and how I acted then. About other things, too, but everything was a prelude to or a consequence of that, and I've left everything in. I've written about you, too, and maybe that will embarrass you. Anyway, you'll just have to take it.

You've asked me several times now why I didn't stay with your mother, and why I treated her as I did. Each time I've answered as best I could, and each time I've seen that you weren't satisfied with what I said. Well, here is another answer. Also unsatisfactory. The odd thing is that what we do to each other just goes into the stream of life, becomes part of that stream, even so, no matter what we intend; and we can remember it or not. This summer, as you and I traveled around together, having our careful good times, I was always remembering. I was terrified, I think, that someday I might not.

July 6, '90

A train for Aigle, in Switzerland. J-M admired my ice axes and asked if I was planning to die in an accident . . . couldn't get a couchette, as they were all taken, so had to reserve a chair, otherwise you stand all the way.

I'm a little depressed this morning. Didn't sleep well. First the mosquitos, few and solitary divebombers in J-M's 3rd-floor flat, just enough of them to keep you awake; then the noise of the occasional car roaring down the street, the sound reverberating with the closeness of the facing buildings.

We've had a good few days. The boy is a full-grown, husky young man with whiskers and hair on his chest. Much thicker through the shoulders than I am. An inch and a half taller. He's been studying for math exams given at the univ. in Brussels, where he's been taking classes for the last 8 months. We joke a lot and crack each other up. His English is remarkable, and he seems happy to have me around and to like me.

What with the jet lag I've felt out of sorts occasionally; two evenings ago, alone because J-M was sleeping over in Brussels, I was quite melancholy going to a movie by myself (*Wilt,* a stupid British comedy not redeemed by being really bad). It feels like the "chemical" depression I've had before, most recently, the first evening at 10,000 feet on a climb on the East Side . . . I'm trying to get all the sun I can to reset my internal clock, and indeed, most of the hours since I flew in have been spent tramping all over Gent.

The city seems busier and a little more prosperous since my visit in '82. I tried to capture my old topographic sense of it but couldn't, and so I'm proceeding on a new and more detailed version aided by my trampings and bike ridings. The traffic is considerably denser and more angry than in '82 — ominous in view of what happened this spring. I often think I see her in the streets, and my depression the night of the movie had much to do with the realization that she really isn't here anymore — that I'm present in her city, which is dense with reminders of her, most particularly in the carriage and appearance of the often exquisite women, but which will not yield her up no matter what. Speaking with J-M at breakfast yesterday I marveled to myself how like his mother's are his beautiful, lucent, black-lashed gray eyes; and then the fact that she was here no more, or here only in this genetic souvenir, came upon me again.

July 17

Woke up this morning in an overheated tent. We're in Tübingen, in the Schwartzwald, staying at a big European-style faire-du-camping place. My week of climbing over. Our tent was once Nicole's and it brings back to me the weeks I spent with her in another (orange-colored, much smaller) tent, in a campground in Fuengirola, on the Costa del Sol. Here J-M was probably conceived.

I had a mild ache of nostalgia as I lay on my mats this morning . . . not nearly so intense as my pneumonia, my diphtheria of nostalgia in '82, when I traveled alone to Paris after seeing J-M and N in Belgium. Then I could hardly walk the streets without an upswelling of feeling and tears, which expressed my hopeless and absurd longing for my younger self, for the Richards of '67, who had traveled Europe so momentously all summer. In '82 I even missed F, the contentious college chum who traveled with me part of the time. I think what I yearned for rather than his somewhat dubious companionship was his perspective on me, his ability to report on who I was back then, the peculiar shape I had . . . This feeling combined with the usual rue at youth gone by, opportunities squandered, superb happiness no longer to be experienced, etc.

That summer we arrived in London just after the 6 Days' War . . . I had argued with my father while staying over in Washington, and he, righteous gentile that he remarkably was, threw me out of the house for my anti-Zionist opinions. I slept in the back seat of his capacious Buick. In London F and I quickly met two sisters and had a place to stay . . . I remember wandering the Vauxhall Bridge road, standing by a statue at a traffic roundabout when a car containing an American couple pulled over to ask directions. Knowing nothing whatsoever F gave them detailed instructions, and as they pulled away in their woeful misinformation a flock of statue-pigeons flew over, drenching him in shit. I was left untouched.

Channel crossing . . . tossing waves, the famous tossing up. Then a train for Paris! The wild upsurge when I heard the conductor actually announce departure in his vraiment français — he was dressed as for a role in a Jacques Tati movie, and I, I was in another, equally silly movie, *The Young American Steps Abroad.* Could it be from this brief ride to Paris that I have a memory of sitting in a clean, sectored railway car and admiring a well-dressed French family, admiring also the well-ordered French countryside in the sundown, which reminded me of something from Hemingway or at any rate, of his own well-ordered, life-hungering responses to the France of his youth? We arrive the Gare du Nord. Find rooms at a hotel recommended in some student guide, on the Left Bank mais certainement. I was later to stumble on this same hotel in '82, to recognize it by the huge chestnut trees lining the block of stolid edifices and also by the ornate grillwork of the balconies . . . everything much cleaner than in '67, the walls white rather than the blackish-gray of memory. Our room was on the sixième étage, the very top. A bidet, the first I'd ever seen, to piss in of course. The hotel looked like something out of the Second Empire, or is it the Third Republic, some insufficiently studied period of 19th-century French history . . . for several nights F and I played poker with the concierge and his young friends; our success encouraged us to imagine ourselves formidable men of parts, flaneurs who might very well support ourselves at the gaming tables of Europe, should it ever "come to that." I went to the Louvre, particularly to the Jeu de Pommes, but I don't recall anything I saw. What I do remember is the streets of the Latin Quarter teeming with students, many of them superb-looking French girls who sat at tiny round tables outdoors, drinking cups of coffee equally tiny, their legs trim under full dark skirts, everything about them piercingly comme il faut, tellement soignée. Maybe I went to the Luxembourg Gardens and the Palais Royale, I don't exactly remember, and I've ever after had a hard time recalling visits to de rigueur tourist attractions.

I lost weight. Sometimes I went all day eating nothing but chocolate bars and bread, with many black coffees to wash it all down. Smoking constantly, Gauloises, Gitanes, Disque Bleu, and in Spain, a kind of black-tobacco cigarette called Celtus I think, three pesetas the pack. Gorging on sense impressions, I hardly needed food to sustain me, and there's a photo of me from the very end of summer, taken by another girl, in a restaurant we found in some remote arrondissement (everything was closed pour les vacances). I stand there broodingly, weighing no more than 145 pounds, displaying my peculiar give-no-quarter expression. Whatever became of those dark glasses, or of the gabardine shirt I wore all that summer, a hand-me-down of my father's, something he wore to putter in the yard? It was painfully precious to me, not only because of its provenance, but because of the "meaning" it palpably contained. Whatever becomes of any of those prized, desperately personal vestments we affect — items as inseparable to our sense of a particular place and time and mood as is the very warp to the weft? I know they disintegrate materially, simply wear out, but what really happens to them — does not their "spirit" persist, return to the ether, to the glowing dome that sustains us all? Some child of the nineties, I hope, will wear my own shimmering garment this summer as he goes and has his own Europe.

From Paris to where? I think F and I split up, preferring to hitchhike by ourselves; we intended to join up later in Spain, at the fiesta de San Fermín. Spain was the real focus of our Europe-lust, Spain and not France, possibly because it seemed less culture-encrusted, less daunting, and also because I had been reading Hemingway for so many years. Also, F was half Latin — his beautiful mother came from Paraguay, a niece or cousin to Stroessner himself — and he spoke a precise, fluent Spanish I envied.

❧

Just returned from a long bike ride by myself. Rode out from Tübingen toward Rottenburg, then north to some other town, everywhere traveling on the network of paved ways exclusive to bike riders and walkers. These southern Germans have some few points. I went up into some orchards. Everything thickly, personally planted, I got the impression of private plots leased over generations by particular families . . . apples, wheat, plums, potatoes, sunflowers, tomatoes, wine grapes; corn, pears, berries, cabbage, kohlrabi growing in ordered abundance, the land looking intensely well husbanded, the variety of crops itself impressive and indicative of a close-to-ground kind of effort. Prolific washes of exuberant wildflowers, their names mostly escape me. Beautiful blue-eyed somethings, wild poppies fearfully red, dandelions, tiny yellows and blues. Huge thickets of pyracantha. The sunflowers in closely planted fields, phototropic heads all aligned . . . the echt forest, which I ventured into on a high ridge above a town, reminded me a bit of Vermont, though not quite so lush — I looked for trolls and felt, at any rate, their recent absence. Now I've returned to the campground, and J-M and I are sitting in folding chairs in front of the green tent. The day has been mostly overcast, with even a little rain — I put on my $200 Gore-Tex slicker for the very first time (never had to wear it climbing). The wind blows at the moment, and the sky is dark gray to the east and lighter elsewhere, blotted by overlayers of hazy cloud. My nose is clear though I was sneezing and blowing throughout my bike journey, all those pollens washing over me . . . I saw many roadside shrines, reminding me of Lawrence's discussion of same during his Alpine walk into Italy. I visited two Catholic graveyards, both clean and repellent, bright with hard, Germanic flowers and shiny gravestones.

J-M looks pensive when I speak of his mother's poetry. Why am I so interested, why now, after so many years? He will try to get me copies if I really want them. The title *Tango Mortale* means nothing to him, he says.

I traveled south from Paris. Did Henry Adams travel by train or coach, or did he also hitch rides, with his hair overgrown and a torn canvas knapsack at his feet? Of all the things of which I was conscious I was not conscious of doing an American thing, of standing in a line, repeating the progress of generations of others . . . In my reduced, inattentive way I was coming to the fabled world of the image, a paradise of color and clever culture. Nothing but prairies behind me — the black, Hawthornian forests, the empty dream. My nineteenth-century ancestors had seen nothing, no museums, no astonishing cathedrals, their eyes were full only of the spooky, doomful American vastness. And then — Paris and Rome. No wonder their travel letters are ecstatic, weirdly incoherent, and that they never want to come home.

Did I not see E, an old college girlfriend, in Geneva? We had broken up only in the middle of the previous year. She was the first girl to consent to sleep with me, and thereafter the object of emotional gambits and derelictions that I think of as my original sexual sin. She worked at the airport, speaking her college German all day. She took me to her dorm-style apartment, a queer replica of the dorm in Pennsylvania where we first made love, and we fucked for days, full of unshed tears and unspoken endearments. Europe made us hot, even Geneva. On the weekend we rented a car and took off into the mountains. I recall sporting along in a Simca 1000, camping and one night even staying at a rustic inn, in a room under the eaves in a bed with down quilts. Barnyard sounds and smells woke us early. E could speak even less easily than I of what she wanted, of what I'd done that hurt her, and I was allowed to impose my stoic-sardonic temperament, my pretend worldliness, so that talking of such things came to seem bad form . . . I could still not believe that someone so intrinsically powerful as compared to me, a blooming, ragingly beautiful young woman, could in any way be at my mercy.

One of her Swiss friends, another worker at the airport, said to her, "I don't understand you Americans . . . When you're angry you say 'Fuck you' to each other, but surely this means 'Make love to you,' and how can this be an expression of anger, a violent thing?"

I went farther south. I remember a hotel room, a grimy city with a railroad station feel. A man picked me up in an old Mercedes, a grizzled pied-noir who had served in the Algerian war, who wanted only to talk about Vietnam. I feared being pilloried for American misdeeds, but he was actually a big hawk, who reproved me instead for my "communist" positions . . . When lunchtime came, all discomforts and disagreements abruptly disregarded, we left the main autoroute and stopped in a little town to buy bread from the baker, vegetables from the greengrocer, meat from the butcher, etc. He drove us out to the woods and made a fire, and we grilled shish kebobs that seemed to me the best things I'd ever eaten. Having drunk some red wine in the heat we dozed against tree trunks. Another driver I remember, a handsome fellow of the Laurence Harvey type, took me to an unprepossessing inn south of a town called Châtillon-en-Diois (why can I remember this, yet not my Social Security number?) and bought me a meal that casually made the point that there can be beauty, balance, even a kind of perfection in all the gestures of a life. I was so happy to order haricots verts, which had figured in a taped dictation from 9th-grade French. Other men also treated me well, did not ask me if I was interested in male sex, if they could only hold my penis, "only hold it," for a moment, as other drivers in the States had done . . . No homosexual has ever tried to overwhelm me, ever bullied me in any way, my brothers-of-a-slightly-different-sex have shown me only courtesy while also displaying a persistent interest, but in the States there is always this odd subtext, especially to any pickup on a highway. Sometimes a darker subtext of course. But I found on these French roads that you really had no good reason to think that the next guy coming round the curve would turn out to be a madman . . . Circling down out of the Massif de Maures, late one clear morning, first glimpse of Nice, the driver and I heard "A Whiter Shade of Pale" for the first time on the car radio. Both thought it "fantastique."

End of June. I don't remember Nice but I was in Cannes, in a cheap hotel on the harbor. I went out to swim among the pleasure craft. At night I had no one to see, nothing connecting me to anyone, I was merely alive and completely free in this slightly overrun, touristic France, which nevertheless offered me shivers of glamour. I celebrated by going to my room and setting a mirror up on a chair, stroking my cock in front of it for about a half hour. The misery of leaving E, the sweetness of leaving, the men who had driven me, the taste of the country they'd wanted me to have, in my obscure hotel room found this expression at least.

On the Spanish border: guardia civil in strange hats showed automatic weapons, listlessly. I walked across. It was a sunny afternoon. I thought of *Homage to Catalonia,* "*a las cinquo de la tarde,*" and El Sordo on his hilltop as the guards yawned and made nothing of me. I don't remember how I got to Pamplona, it may have been on a bus. I arrived after heavy rains.

> July 21. We have rushed back to Gent from southern Germany, seven hours driving nonstop so that J-M could go to work at 5 P.M. in his taxi. Gent is utterly different from two weeks ago. Then it was cold, Novemberish, but now the air is unbearably heavy. I roamed the streets till 2 A.M. seeking relief, so uncomfortably warm that I had to take off my socks and undershirt and stuff them in my pockets. There is a music fest in progress and in the centrum stages have been set up every fifty yards or so, and all manner of bands are performing for an enormous crowd of confused-looking Belgians, who drink gallons of beer but never seem to get drunk, only more red in the cheek. My favorite band last night was a tango ensemble con-

sisting of piano, guitars, accordion, contrabass, and violin. The violinist was a woman of about 25, with a wide face and a bizarre, insinuating smile, who wore a sort of '20s velvet hat, plum-colored, that I badly wanted to stroke. She played with intense vibrato and brought off complex pizzicato passages with delirious aplomb, and afterward she smiled at the audience as if deeply, objectively pleased by the music as well as by herself. This morning I arose around 9 and went out into the hazy, hot streets again to buy rolls and eggs and a loaf of dark bread containing walnuts. Also mint tea, milk in a box, and a handful of bananas almost perfectly ripe, speckled like yellow trout. It's now past noon and J-M hasn't awakened yet, so I must eat all by myself. The apartment smells of slumbering men.

❧

There were hundreds, nay thousands, of tourists camped out at a sordid, muddy park on the near outskirts. I met up with F who was staying in the park, but I refused to camp in mud and instead found a room in the back of a house, a kind of slave-quarters apartment. In the center of town was a fountain, perhaps the same one Hemingway describes as running red with vinous vomit after a few days of fiesta. We sat at a café outdoors in a dusty street and ordered wine. Other tourists, of a few more years than ours, sat at tables nearby and contrived to look like groupings of Jake, Brett, Mike, Robert Cohn, and so forth, their impersonations quite startling and only called into question by there being so many of them. One chap indeed looked just like Hem aged 58 or so, whitening beard and confused stare and all. F and I bought beautiful goatskin botas, disappointingly lined with plastic, and filled them at huge casks in a bodega. Oh, but it was a real relive *The Sun*–type fiesta, except that we had no women as I recall, and we couldn't hobnob with matadors, and the whole scene was so grossly overrun with others trying to act out the same script as to cause a warp from willed unreality in the very air.

The corridas were second rate, staged only for tourists, I expect. Yet I liked them and went several times. I saw El Cordobés one long afternoon, also other, stiffer, nobler workers of the bull. The plaza de toros seemed enormous from the outside, and there was a delicious glamour in buying sol y sombre tickets at the little booths, just as Jake et al. had done in fictional 1924 or so. Inside, the plaza seemed small, intimate. Although a few days later, when I finally got up the courage to "run with the bulls" a little (actually just join the crowd on the arena floor as some bored-looking bulls and steers trotted out among us), the plaza seemed huge again, and I hardly came near a bull nor one near me.

I was reading Kafka stories as I recall. I remember in particular "Gregor Samsa awoke one morning after uneasy dreams," which peculiar phrase I read sitting in the sun on a crumbling stone wall, conscious of my poetic surroundings, also of my admirable refinement, to be reading such a famous phrase which Nabokov somewhere remarks on account of those "uneasy dreams," so casually-portentously mentioned.

A few days on, as per the instructions in *The Sun,* I took off for the country to the east, to the Irati River area. Here Jake and Mike went to fish for a few days, and here I also went though alone. The river was low and seemed too hot for carp, let alone trout. I caught nothing, never had a bite, although I had fun buying a cheap rod and reel and then going into the hills by bus. I stayed in a riverside inn and though I could not eat "the trout I had caught myself," I did eat and sleep well, very well. Tramping along the Irati late one morning I ran into a pudgy young Spaniard also with rod in hand, and for some reason it struck me that he was also trying to live out some absurd script (certainly, it was too close to noon for either of us to be serious about fishing). We tried to converse, I in my high school French, he in lisping Castilian, and we shook hands finally with some kind of embarrassed understanding achieved.

On to Madrid. Arrival early in the morning in a sports car driven by a bearded man, and the city seeming to rise up from a roundish valley, through which we careeringly traveled. I asked to be taken to the old quarter directly, where F and I had agreed to rendezvous should that prove possible. We did meet again, and I went to stay with him in a third-floor pension (may it actually have been named Pension La Pena, as I now recall with a feeling of almost-certainty?) that provided dormlike accommodations and was very bright inside, with tall white and yellow painted walls and crisp white sheets everywhere, sort of like a clinic. By now I was probably reading *The Magic Mountain,* that earnest massif of literate argumentation which Nabokov warns us to disdain, which I eagerly devoured. I went to the Prado as on a religious pilgrimage, and I loved most and best the virile, cartoony Goyas, in particular the series of prints on the horrors of war. One composition, of many people in a frightening mob, had the form of a giant rat, it seemed to me — I tried to explain my perception to another onlooker, a Danish student, who taught me the Spanish word *ratone* in response.

I remember being amazed by the handsome oils in the stairwell down to the men's room. Hemingway had ordered me to go to the Prado, I think, he may even have advised me to like Goya this much, but even so I did go, I was amazed, something authentic emerged from this complex, boyish wash of pretensions and self-performances I think.

Somehow I've forgotten — I was on the Costa Brava before, the week before Madrid, in a crumby seaside town. I went there directly from Pamplona. The towns looked cheesy and kitschy to me (although I didn't know the word *kitsch* yet, it was Nicole who was to teach me), I had a room up a narrow, foul-smelling staircase near a beach. My first night I dutifully went to a bar and drank several Pernods, as per the instructions in *A Moveable Feast,* marveling as per further instructions at the milky melding of fluids when the liquor was mixed with water, and soon I had to hurry home to moan and vomit half the night. But next day I seem to be out on the dirty, steep plage, where I display myself in my skimpy black tank suit, Thomas Mann in hand. I was smoking harsh, unfiltered Spanish cigarettes by now (the taste of these and of Gauloises pursues me even now, provokes the memory of Europe, particularly France circa 1967, sometimes when I was a student in Berkeley I would buy a pack for old times' sake, only to come down with a sore throat or a cold soon enough). (I remember one afternoon in Pamplona, F and I went into a tobacconist's and he bought a pack of 1-x-2 cigarettes, pronounced "Une-equis-dos," from a dark pretty girl who asked if he would be running with the bulls the next day. "Clearly," he replied, "and so I may be dead tomorrow," and I envied his false nonchalance, his robust Spanish once again.) Out on the beach, on the dirty Costa Brava beach, in my thin and droopy tank suit, well tanned probably, thinner than I'd been in my adult life, well built for all that and no doubt attractively unshaven, with a bush of dark, rough wavy hair which stood out from my head like the image of "intensity," my excess of young man's vibrancy, I met a pretty woman with honey-colored skin and brown hair, possibly a German, possibly a Swede. We flirted and sat together for a while, and I remember the seduction was going quite well until she asked how old I was, and I replied truthfully. Then she seemed only amused, and she left me posthaste, and I was sorely disappointed with myself for this uncharacteristic descent into truth-telling.

When I was in Madrid, though — well, I was really lonely. This despite the Prado and F, despite our homey pension and the restaurant we ate at every night (thirty pesetas a plate), the real reason to be in Europe was to meet women, wasn't it, to have love to have sex, all the other realities of traveling and seeing and eating and being were as nothing compared to this, to the intensity of affairs, only these carried the real conviction of living, of doing something large and adult, "fatal." I liked sex I know but even more I liked or was compelled by the feeling of being alive, with my face pressed up against the true pulsing maw of things; I had this feeling most vividly, perhaps exclusively, when I was in bed with a woman, entering an exciting, excited woman's beauty and thereby feeling my own.

I was lonely, I say; and one day I went wandering along the outskirts of a park, where I found a grillwork building with several tables set out on a patio. I remember that the place seemed like an island, maybe narrow lanes of roadway passed it on every side. Sitting at one of these tables, writing postcards calmly, deliberatingly, was one of the most beautiful women I had ever seen, I try to remember her now as she was in her exotic, healthful young-womanhood, not as Nicole, because the almost barbaric quality of her beauty arrested me, shocked me, and it has always after seemed different from the real her, unconnected to her core which, as far as I ever got to know it, was a formidably strong, self-denying thing, a sort of soul-fortress.

I saw her, and I was immediately terrified: as any beautiful woman used to terrify me, for good reason. I walked on by. But I was lonely, I had been without a girl since Switzerland, and if I didn't have the courage to approach a beautiful woman now, in my 21st year, in my Madrid summer and my handsomeness and hunger, then when would I ever have it and why should I care for myself, how did I have the right to regret my loneliness, if I was without the courage to try to cure it? I went back and sat down carefully. Maybe I asked her if I could borrow a pen, maybe I asked where she had gotten the postcards. She looked up.

❧

About 11 A.M. I slept poorly last night on a thin mattress on J-M's floor, the Gent mosquitoes bedeviling me terribly despite some pesticide device he plugs into the wall socket. R, a friend from the university, slept on the couch. R has been thrown out by his Dutch girlfriend, he tells us. He laughs and describes her pique when he failed to show up for his qualifying exams in physics, thus rendering nugatory seven years of preparation. R has a father in distant America, just like J-M; he has never met his father, they've never corresponded. I've been feeding him and buying him medicine and new clothes, in a pathetic attempt to make something up to him, I suppose (and to J-M, and to all sons of abandoning fathers everywhere), and last night while J-M drove his taxicab downtown, R and I went to the music fest together, to this tiresome, somnambulistic event that goes on forever.

There were loud combustions just past midnight — the Belgian 4th of July. Seeing the hordes of festing, music-appreciating Belgians does little for me; they look dull and peevish, vaguely out of sorts and out of place. The men become egg-shaped as they age, I see. They aren't rowdy, though, in their crowds; and they do seem to enjoy themselves moderately. The German faces I saw in the Schwartzwald were more interesting, more captivating by far. The public pool where J-M and I swam every day in Tübingen was like a set out of *Triumph of the Will,* a vast, classic-looking installation, Olympic-size pool (fifty meters) set in acres of lawn, momentous shower and locker facilities, hundreds of young Germans all the time strutting about in their health and knowingness. But give me a German girl, I decided, this will always be my first choice: one with about a thousand years of sex-intelligence, of desire and sex-disdain encoded in her haughty, structural face. The features are not fine, nor are they exactly coarse; merely hard and strange, at least to eyes like mine. Lots of sun-browned, softly gleaming skin like the crust of white-bread loaves. Hair more often honey-colored than flaxen.

❧

We sat at neighboring tables for a while, talking in English. Then we may have walked somewhere. She was staying at a "camping," she said, somewhere on the outskirts of town. We agreed to meet at a cantina that night, where flamenco was to be performed. She was mad about flamenco, I learned later, and I, myself, was generally Spain-mad, glad to extend my enthusiasm to yet another form. I remember returning to the pension in the old quarter and describing my discovery to F, who wished me further "good hunting," and later that night I sought out the bar-theater she had named, and I was initially crushed to see that she had indeed shown, but with another young man as escort. But we all sat at a table together, drank some wine, and somehow I displaced him. I believe the attraction that night was a dancer called Rosa Duran — she was a small, unbeautiful, hard-limbed Andalusian a bit on in years, who could indeed dance magically. Or maybe I'm conflating things; Nicole was mad for this Duran, and maybe we didn't see her that first night at the first theater, only later, somewhere to the south. The connection had been made, in any case, an attraction felt. When did I first walk with her out to her camping, could it have been that first night? A few days later, I actually dared to kiss her. I knew it needed to be done, just because she was making it so difficult; I wanted to, of course, and yet I also feared it, and I seem to have managed it standing up against a post, in the evening shadows at her campground. Her exquisite face smelled of apricots and roses.

I must have begun lying to her immediately. Sharply cognizant of my disappointment on the Costa Brava, I told her I was 25 and then, since I claimed to be beyond college age, had to fabricate a career: I was a "writer," I said, I had published a few stories, maybe a book was in the offing. She seemed to like all this and I was continually astonished that such a ravishing woman would let me kiss her, that she seemed to have warmed toward me.

❧

July 25. Very full, good day, so fine I didn't feel it quite — that is, my feelings of it were not quite as intense as "it" was. J-M sleeping in, I went out around 8:30 and had petit déjeuner and rented a bike from a nice lady at the tourism office in Die, then rode about 5 km east and north through corn and sunflower fields to arrive at the Pas de la Roche, a narrow corner in the road with rock walls on both sides. Many climbing routes had been put up, and I had hopes of finding a partner but failed. Left my bike chained to a bridge railing and admired the walls for a while (a French guy was teaching some Dutch kids how to climb), then began hiking up a narrow path through woods. I had an excellent if dated topo map, and it led me toward Serré Jean, an ancient farmstead, through low pine and oak forest where, turning some corners of the path, I was stupefied by the utter silence of things, the perfect late-morningness. Profusion of wildflowers in the broken shade. I felt spiritually waked up somehow, the ancientness affected me, none of the trees stood taller than about 25 feet yet the forest was clearly virgin growth, an ur-stand of some sort. I reached Serré Jean and turned reluctantly back downhill, toward the Abbaye de Valcroissant (est. 1188). The building massive and stony and quietly old, there were beehives and no monks and someone was harvesting round bales of hay. The arches off the interior courtyard looked Roman, there were simple, multipaned leaded windows clumsily stained piss-yellow. I had to begin my big hike now, I went east from the abbey and took a remarkable shit in the woods, the trails were strangely, confusingly marked and I was never sure I was on the right one till I'd climbed several hundred meters into forest, reaching some crossing indicated on my map. I found grasshoppers with blood-red interior wings in the meadows; skinks, lizards, and salamanders, which brought to mind the late Bulle Ogier; the profusion of wildflowers alluded to above, now augmented by lavender and black-purple and buttery blooms; huge, finely woven spider webs, with a funnel trap in the center of each, set out on the bushes like linen drying. The forest went up and up, and I too went up and up, a fine quiet forest it was (except for a family of Dutch that climbed below me, their fluting voices rising) grown on an intimate scale, with many plants strongly resembling New World varieties, but the forest, taken as a whole, different in its soul, differently mysterious, cunning, playfully threatening. I had eaten a lunch of cheese, cucumber, and bread after my remarkable shit near the abbey, and now I kept on gradually climbing for an hour or more. I headed for the Col Ménil, then detoured toward the Col Fouchard, which I reached probably around noon. To make the col I passed through an area indicated on the map by the name Le Paradis, and indeed, it had an Elysian feeling, with bee-humming meadows and rocky open spaces and patches of low forest alternating, views down toward the abbey and to farm valleys in the west available at every turn of path. I drank from a seep feeding a tiny waterfall, having to climb down rock steps almost to the very precipice itself (where the thin run of water cascaded casually over a rock lip). The water was sweet, really like an un-dry wine, not very cold. On my return in the direction of l'abbaye and the Pas de la Roche I encountered myriad butterflies (they seemed to be out in greatest numbers at the lower elevations, in spangled shade), veritable flotillas and swooning fleets of flutterers, species all intermingled, leopard-spotted and black-and-white-spotted and dark purple blacks and some whose coloring was like yellowed manuscript — I imagined their wing markings told stories. Close to the Pas de la Roche, two enormous butterflies, starkly black and white, mated repeatedly just in front of me. Meeting in the air, they would flutter to the ground, where one spread its wings flat while the other stood in avid attendance. Suddenly this desperate, sincere-looking butterfly-fucking sparked something in me, and I went up a closely grown hillside, took off my shorts, and there stroked my old, tired but yearning penis in a bed of moist blue flowers.

July 26. Didn't sleep well last night, though I was well and truly tired after my forest trek. I dropped the rental bike into a stream unlocking it uncarefully from a bridge railing; bent the rear wheel, wobbled back to Die. Then I had a moral crisis over whether to tell the rental lady, show her what I'd done to her poor bike. Finally I did and got her to keep 50F of my deposit money, still, I'm a little troubled, thinking the whole rear wheel may have to be replaced, which will cost much more. But one can worry (I allowed myself to conclude) about such things no end, it becomes an indulgence at some point, to obsess over one's moral spotlessness, especially in small matters; just to the extent I feel spotty in the larger ways,

I worry and pick at all the little things, morosely. The day was so superb, the forest so Edenic and generous to me, I felt unworthy even as I devoured its moments. It has always been my method, though, to obsess, to doubt and question, then to become fed up, to barge ahead like an utter greedy ruffian, somehow frightened most by the prospect of a fall into endless moral qualm. I think in this connection of Rick S., Rosemarie's old lover, who makes a career of being spotless, absolutely beyond moral question and "fine" almost in the Jamesian sense. Yet he seems to me a withheld, sexless, repressed sort of man — his fires utterly quenched at age 29 or so.

But I am tired this morning, I am. It's 11:30 now, and J-M has his precious diesel Rabbit off at the garage, where they're to fix a slave-cylinder. I immensely enjoyed our two days/nights together in this clean, modest, 2-star hotel — we had a little garden just outside the window, also a little pool and a patio nearby, from which one had an unobstructed view over tout les toits de Die, a marvelous old Roman-French cubist effect. My stomach has been troubling me, I think I've been drinking too much wine. Or maybe it's my bike rental worry. The day is fleece-soft, agreeably warm, with a clean sky.

July 28 1 A.M. Have been in Paris since last night, by myself. Today I hiked near the Gare du Nord and finally found a hotel not too dégoûtant, costing a mere 145F, about twice what I expected to pay. Prices of everything are shocking compared to '82, when we enjoyed a stronger dollar. As I got off the metro at St.-Germain-des-Prés I braced myself for a return of the nostalgia that hit me like a case of typhus in '82 — it did not recur, and I've so far been walking the streets feeling them to be part of a big, grimy city, which just happens to be Paris, where I happened to spend some time in my youth, which I don't have to recall if I don't want.

Went to the Musée d'Orsay in the afternoon. Superb Cézannes, Manets, Sisleys, one Bonnard I think was my favorite of the whole collection: a man in a boat (I think it's called "Le Passeur") looking across a river to cultivated fields and woods, the fields somehow suggesting the whole world or worlds of the imagination. I've been reading *Robinson Crusoe* these last couple of weeks, and it intrigued me to find a painting ("Le Mort d'Orphée," by one Eugène Levy, school of Ingres) because in Crusoe there is some talk of killing and eating sea turtles, yet no mention of using the shells as bowls or barrels or anything else; in the painting, however, Orpheus' lyre is made of a dark tortoise shell, and this for some reason shocked me, perhaps because I've gotten used to Crusoe turning every material to every conceivable use. The women abusing poor dead or dying Orph are quietly, intensely enjoying their murderous play, and the hero himself is unmistakably a pale young Jew, black curly hair and dark brows, very like my own image — or maybe it's the artist's image of himself.

Paris much more diverse now. But why are the blacks, even these European blacks, always required to be the poor ones, always condemned to live in the most sordid streets? Tonight on the metro in a car full of sub-Saharan Africans I thought, "They're disadvantaged as to modernity, that's all — they're an ancient, imponderable race, yet somehow they can't ever get on the forward edge. Their magnificence does not translate." What they're good at modernity chooses not to value. I was riding in the direction Clignancourt.

July 28, noon. Maintenant je suis dans un café et je bu (?) une tasse de thé menthe . . . This practically exhausts my French. Actually at a party last night I talked at some great length and was complimented on my command of the language, I think some French are astonished to meet an American who can speak at all. But I know my limitations, linguistically and in other ways. I converse comfortably only about obvious things, I have no acquaintance with the subjunctive, my future is vague, my past messy.

It rained this morning, a shocking cold thunderstorm. I sat in my room not able to feel the romance of it, worried only about my lack of both raincoat and umbrella, about how I was missing petit déjeuner downstairs. Aside from my love of French and my desire to speak it, I feel more routinely American than ever before, not eager anymore to be taken for something else. Now my language reveries all run in the direction of finding equivalencies, for example, a Frenchman's horrid, characteristic mangling of English has its correspondence in my torturing of his own language, and both distortions aren't such a crime, after all . . . When I was younger, a bold traveler here and in Latin America, I hated most to be taken for an American, made for what I so painfully was. But those were the days of U.S. megapreponderance in the world, when I earnestly believed we had much to feel guilty about (we still do, but not exclusively, not just we Americans). Now I feel even in this short trip how far we've fallen, how rapidly America subsides (and toward what); who knows but that our collapse will continue and we will soon be truly third rate, even economically. One pleasant consequence is we don't seem to be so intensely resented anymore.

After the storm, I made my way up the Rue du Fauborg-St.-Martin, a lively, vibrant big-city street, to R. Louis-Blanc to Blvd. de la Chapelle, where I found a crazed plein-aire Arab market in vegetables and shoddy clothes. Absolutely packed with shoppers, 90% of them North African, and the hawkers shouting in urgent, almost hysterical tones suggesting imminent violence, but intended only to create excitement, to startle us into buying.

The concentric arches pattern of the paving stones. I'm in a street near Sacré-Coeur, but I remember the cathedral as a heavy, unspiritual sort of edifice, Notre-Dame as built by the New Deal, and I don't much want to visit. The air is muggy after the rain. My ankles hot in wool socks — I've rolled the tops down. Eight years ago I saw some leatherwork sold by an Arab on the steps of Sacré-Coeur, the peculiar redness of the bag or was it a jacket attracted me strongly, I stared a bit too long. The Arab vendor, a handsome and desperate-looking fellow, pursued me down the steps. We were suddenly in *The Roman Spring of Mrs. Stone,* or was it *Death in Venice,* taking a page or two from *L'Immoraliste.* One's economic superiority vis-à-vis such a person makes it hard to have an even-tempered encounter, to state the obvious . . . But why did that dark, freshly worked, deeply red leather attract me so, except as a symbol of the man himself?

The sun has come out. It illumines the stone wall opposite my café.

Musée de Montmartre. It cost 20F to enter and I long deliberated, ruing this wholesale descent into tourism. An old charming building, with a courtyard full of trees (one prune-plum in fruit) through which you pass to the museum proper. Various paintings by second-rate Montmartre artists of the last 200 years, plus good stuff as well, mainly old illustrations, posters, decorations from the walls of Le Chat Noir, etc. Works of Dufy, Utrillo, Modigliani, Bernard. The study of Charpentier (musician/composer) recreated behind glass. I don't know why but I suffered a short sharp attack of nostalgia sickness here, it began with an old photo of some deserted Montmartre street corner in winter, and I felt the pulse of that old time and the art to be created in those streets. Winter, après les touristes. Another shot from about 1963 showed a girl bundled up against November weather hurrying down a little square — just her quick ankle out of focus. This thin ankle made me want to cry with the sense of that time, that specific afternoon and instant now lost, all the possibility of it; when one is young one lives in "exemplary" fashion I saw, as if each act proves that one will be able to live just this way, on into an indefinite future; when you begin to age you're no longer proving anything, certainly not that you'll be able to live in a certain way, and the future is less endless and the moments are only of themselves, full of consciousness of their briefness. I think I become nostalgic thinking of my promise and energy and the great work I might have done, but which I seem to have lost the thread of . . . Oh, to feel that sense of possibility, sense dependent on an essential ignorance of life, an incomplete self-discovery.

The artists of Montmartre reflected only their place — this is all they felt they had to do. There are literally thousands of street scenes, good and bad, and one feels the multiplicity and the rough beauty of life in those streets, absolutely. The pleasure just of reflecting any reality: any creation is a kind of homage, I guess, to the Great Creator and his work, a sharing of the feeling at the original moment . . . The thought begins to elude me.

Somehow I don't remember how limited, how crippled, I was in my youth — psychologically wounded, frail, afraid of going mad — I've had to work and grow, become more sturdy, to be able to indulge these feelings of hopeless loss and passionate yearning for the "old times."

Modigliani Room, Musée de Montmartre. Just one substantial oil painting, I guess they were lucky to get even that. It took courage to draw and paint as he did, there's so little going on in his canvases that he must have been constantly ridiculed. Verging on the overstark and the clumsy, like Monet. I saw a photo of his wife, Jeanne Hébuterne, then understood his characteristic female heads: she had the retroussé inexpressive eyes, the nose with a thick bridge all the way down. He, in several photos, was quite a handsome Jewish-Italian type with dark, penetrant gaze.

In Switzerland this summer I saw posters everywhere, advertisements for a huge retrospective — on street corners, in restaurants, on buses, in shop windows always the nude, yearning, contorted torso of Jeanne (who threw herself out of a window three days after Modigliani died), the pale thatch of her pubis so real one tastes the sea flavor.

July 29. Day all blue and fresh-washed. I've bought a ticket for the Brussels train leaving 14:45.

I was exhausted from walking all day yesterday, only wanted to eat well and then to bed. Settled on a dark brasserie called Voyages opposite the Louis-Blanc metro stop, Blvd. de Faubourg-St.-Martin. Absolutely packed with chic people mostly in their thirties, an amazing percentage with strong, avid faces. Several parties of diners included one black, a kind of fashion statement perhaps. The men wear their hair like hoods of the fifties, or more exactly, like proto-longhairs of 1963 or so, sideburns but no grease, etc. I caught the eye of a woman with a strong, un-made-up face, we flirted distantly all during my repast. Sleepy eyes, dark brows, and a haggard look, the whole troubled world somehow implicated in her expression. Doleful consciousness of time. I thought, "How can I be her consolation, why can't she stop looking at me — my attention, my sexual recognition of her, must be an antidote to something, her face says that our fate is bleakly certain, our condition hopeless, for that reason desperate gestures are allowed." I thought of R just at the moment of orgasm, or just an instant before, sweet, steely-complaisant R, the look she has, it moves me down to my heels sometimes, her crisis the human crisis, with love I carry her across. I see fate in women, mostly. I doubt they see it mostly in us. The woman now stands up, she's rather tall, at least as tall as me, and looks at me frankly. Her boyfriend hurries to pay the waiter. They walk out.

City jammed, swarming, teeming with tourists. I don't remember anything of the kind before, certainly not in '82. The world has changed. I don't mind.

It's Sunday, however, and the streets outside the centers of activity are deserted. The Musée de Picasso on the Rue Thorigny is hidden in a quiet spot, only a small complement of tourists have made their way here, mostly by taxi. Not all that much of Picasso on display when you consider his astonishing output over 75 years, but it's agreeably well organized as to period and so forth. I noticed the largest, most intensely attentive groups around the displays of contemporary photographs, "Picasso at his atelier Le Bateau-Lavoire with his mistress so-and-so," etc. This perhaps has something to do with his rigorous abstracting and leaching away from his art everything anecdotal and, well, of interest, so that his old fiercely moderne creations now seem just sort of bloodless and ungiving, too simple. Some nice stuff, though; I liked in particular a naked family on a beach, father mother and child with privates demurely obscured, their skin the most gorgeous colorist pink; in reproductions this never shows through, and the point of the thing is lost. I also liked some late tauromachia engravings–paintings–line drawings, the fierce powerful frightening bullheads also strangely wistful — monsters wanting a caress. Picasso reminds me of Dostoevsky because he's capable of giving you a reflection of life which you can enter and dream in, but he almost never does — he's after different game, "ideas" or something, and I for one feel deprived. I suppose I'm hopelessly on the anecdotal/materialist side of things.

Now leaving Paris from the Gare du Nord; the train began moving gently and almost silently five seconds ago, with no announcement.

I read in the papers that production of the Citroën 2CV (Deux Cheveaux) has finally halted, as of about July 27. This was the sort of small, underpowered, toy-tank-like car in which Nicole and I toodled around Spain 23 years ago. And now J-M owns another 2CV, one that also belonged to his mother, which he must sell as part of her estate. He too has fond memories of taking vacations with her in it . . . Once they went to the Boden See together, and the little car labored pathetically up the Black Forest hills, he says, nearly expiring en route.

Last night before my flight, J-M and I went out to Ypres, to his grandmother's house. She's a warm-seeming, emptily jolly lady in her late seventies. Lives in an apartment packed with knickknacks and '50s-style plush furniture. Her two sisters, also widows, live nearby. They hosted our dinner which consisted of platters of meat, seafood, and vegetables ordered in from a local restaurant. The three old ladies are not visibly in mourning. The grandmother talked of Nicole once or twice, explaining that she had not understood her daughter so well, they had not been close. "But she was one's child after all." The younger aunt, whom the others call La Petite, got tipsy on good champagne and fairly ogled me and made much of my curly hair (as J-M had predicted she might). La Petite was the mistress of the richest man in Ypres for many years, and when he died she inherited 18 properties among other things. The grandmother is the least well off, I think, the two others quite rich.

Don't know why I feel so cranky toward them — so unforgiving. (And what have I to forgive?) They were kind to me, much as Nicole was always kind, and they evidently dote on J-M. I visited each in her home as we drove about rounding them up for dinner, one gave me plum preserves she had put up herself, plus a plastic bag of haricots verts. The smells in these houses were such as I've never encountered before: pleasant, musty, domestic smells but incommensurable, quintessentially foreign. Ypres is the town in Flanders where untold thousands of British and others died in WWI . . . After dinner J-M and I drove out to Proutem, N's ancestral village, where her urn is buried in a grave beside her beloved father's. I remembered coming to the village with her in '82 . . . Somehow my impression then was of a backward farm community far and gone in the flat fields; in fact the town has several prosperous streets, a small cathedral, au courant–looking shops and a general air of modernity. The graveyard behind a lesser church. Gleaming tombstones, great weight of marble, everything immodest. So this is where you end up, my dear. I remembered the fragrant skin of the young beauty I knew in Spain, who would still from time to time get blemishes near her absurdly perfect mouth . . . I didn't like the graveyard, I had no words to say, and J-M and I quickly satisfied ourselves there.

We made plans to leave Madrid together — to travel south. There was her 2CV to go in, and we packed her tent and my few belongings and took off. I remember the car so low-geared and yet underpowered that it felt like a windup toy, especially going up hills; the shift was in the middle of the dash, an arrangement I'd never seen before, it took a while to get used to. One night we slept off the road, hardly bothering to make camp, just tumbling out on the ground. We didn't make love and we hadn't so far, and I was happy, I was happy. I anticipated it of course — felt it to be inevitable. But she wanted to go slow, she wanted me to "prove" something about myself, my fundamental decency, I suppose, my seriousness about her. (And yet she liked my insouciance, I know — my braggart American roughness, which hardly promised tenderness.) It was a poetic, a tensely tender dream of love we had: talking about Lorca as we drove, "*a las cinquo de la tarde,*" and she would translate her own poems, full of blood imagery (I secretly graded her down for this). At some point I learned that she was still a virgin at twenty-seven — I don't remember doubting this for even a moment, and later I was to have the classic evidence (blood imagery again). She was a delicate, slow-handed, fruit-and-rose-scented young woman, vulnerable and alert, yet withal a composed, dignified, anciently knowledged European, a sort of icon in my eyes.

She liked to have demure, even-tempered fun, could sometimes be made to laugh, though she never really let go and was incapable, I think, of either ecstasies or hysterics. I remember late one afternoon, the Spanish heat and the sun just gone behind hills, we wound up some road in first gear and then down a steep grade, and she recited a soliloquy from *Yerma* for me, followed by a poem of her own, which commented on it. She knew how to camp, how to bathe in the rivers, to buy fruits and cheeses of the country, everything done with a certain consciousness, aesthetically and spiritually, and in a way I was in touch with a version of the Hemingway discovery, that of the European real, real food, real wine, bread bought at the dusty baker's shop, the world recognized for what it was because seen slowly, with full attention. She hated "kitsch," denounced it constantly, and consequently loved all that advertised itself as being natural. (But wait, let me take back that suggestion, that snide intimation in the phrase "advertised itself," as if the world were somehow promoting itself, putting itself over on her, exploiting some sentimental delusion. She was basically not susceptible to flummery, not to any but my own, and she saw things for what they were, touched the world and found it good and whole.)

We stopped at the Alhambra. Hot hot day. Moorish arches and overelaborate tilework, I remember walking around "aesthetically," sensing that my response to this place was significant and therefore so was I, a cocksure, half-delirious 21-year-old traveling with an older woman, a beauteous poet; our courtship lent drama to the afternoon. She was almost overcome by the heat, we had to seek water in a dusty courtyard. She talked about her fragility even then, in a tone of surprise or amusement.

We had traveled well together. A sexual feeling, we

often kissed and lay together for hours, still we didn't make love, the feeling was so conscious, intense. We arrived in the South. First we went to Fuengirola, then a little beach settlement southwest of Málaga. It happened that my parents were also traveling in Spain that month, camping only kilometers away, at a hotel in Torremolinos. Ray Wendt, my father's Alabama army buddy, had come along too, with his bibulous wife, Sharon. (Probably my father paid for their tickets.) When Ray first laid eyes on Nicole, I remember, he practically began to salivate, and a threatening, southern-redneck-rapist look crossed his face — a kind of tribute I guess. I had told her so many half-truths by then, about my family, my education, my adventures, that I anticipated this encounter with some anxiety. "You must be so proud of Abel — please tell me about his books." I steered all conversation away from such pertinent subjects, largely by virtue of my urgent intensity — I was really doing it then, far gone, completely overboard in my impersonation of a poetic, harshly glamorous young artist, the roughneck lover, beautiful fatal boy.

Excellent dinners. The Hotel Riviera built out over the Mediterranean, scarily cantilevered, and fifteen years later I was to read that it had fallen in, with loss of life. Several swimming pools, one built right beside a sunken piano bar, through whose portholed walls you peered into blue-green depths. One afternoon Nicole took a dip, and Ray led me down and ordered me a bourbon, and as we watched her undulate past the portholes he asked if I had ever considered how many miles my cock had traveled — miles inside of women, that is. Seven inches or so per stroke, so and so many strokes per act, how many miles, how many dozens or even hundreds of miles . . .

My father, gracious as always. My mother was deeply fearful, she saw our attraction and was terrified that this older, Catholic woman would get her claws into me, the barely fledged Jewish scion. Even so my parents offered us a room of our own, a balconied room on an upper floor; and it was here, in these cushy digs, in the Hotel Riviera, that the blood of maidenhood was finally spilled, on an ecru sheet with a little starch. Then began a period of catch-up ball; we returned to Fuengirola, to our crowded campground, and I remember sleeping late one morning, the tent heating up uncomfortably, making love over and over, finally I tumbled out to encounter the French couple of the tent next door, who had heard us all night and were simply fed up, sans blague. Nicole, this exotic beauty, this veritable goddess, whom I'd been dreaming of for weeks, if not all my life, was strangely like girls I'd known before — her femaleness, her flavor, what seemed to please her (I had no well-developed idea of this, I must have caused few, if any, frissons in my first five years of being a lover), all was oddly like what I'd encountered before, and I think I was disappointed. The sex spell was on us, however, and I was the agent of a certain marked change in her — she took part, as I recall, with a kind of detachment, vaguely amused by this pell-mell tumbling down of walls, but take part she did.

One night, forcing ourselves to get out of the tent, we went to a nearby restaurant, a rowdy night spot organized around the *corrida* theme. A small bullring, wooden stands, and after dinner the male patrons were encouraged to go a few passes with a stunted, skinny-haunched animal with shortened horns. I had told Nicole of a certain "bullfighting past" of mine — I'd trained in Mexico, in the state of Chihuahua, been a *novillero* before taking the *alternativa,* who knows what utter, shameful nonsense I professed . . . How can she have believed this, I must credit her open-heartedness, her fairness, but also I know that a spell was on me, in response to this felt need to fascinate, to compel and seduce with words, and a power awoke in me. (But this has always been the case: becoming what I pretend, not a bullfighter, but a storyteller, which is what I'd been claiming all along. Just as I'd become, pretending to be a suitable romantic object, her actual seducer.) Being with Nicole, with this real, live woman, engaged in an actual affair, fired me with an absurd daring, but by no means was I getting in that bullring, not with a wild animal, horns and hooves and all that. Flat chickened out, as in Pamplona. I invented some excuse, probably raging against the "inferior" conditions, the animal's malformations, etc., and she appeared to believe me.

Another night: we go to a theater to see *A Man and a Woman,* Trintignant and Anouk Aimée in their moods, drenched in saccharine. Nicole guiltily liked the thing, while I denounced it vigorously, in my disabused, college wise-guy way. Just this last year I saw it again, in Redwood City, and embarrassed myself with public weeping — and it's still the same crap.

Late August. Taking a trip to Gibraltar, Algeciras and Jerez. The famous apes, cars making a traffic-throb before the Rock. I felt tired, drained, dreamy. I was even a little bored, I think. Had carried out the great seduction, and now the desired object, the yielding and fragrant captive, no longer scintillated quite so. Life demanded that we spend mere time together, after all; and there was a problem with maintaining, from her side, the poetic/romantic intensity and from mine, the sexually dangerous/romantic. Or maybe I had somehow "ruined" her, as the morality tales would have it, debased her with my lies and sexual overkill . . . I was maintaining, I think, so many poses and false fronts all at once it's no wonder I felt exhausted. The traffic, and we, finally moved past the checkpoint.

She was fine. Lovely in all her responses. We stayed several nights at sordid hotels, and her tenderness glowed against the stained walls. Somehow I'd brought her down, to the level of one of my college conquests . . . She wore her long, heavy hair parted in the middle; for her it wasn't a style but just the right way to wear it, a northern European way, and it happened to coincide with the Joan Baez–y coiffure then in fashion back in the States. Her poetic, Madonna-ish uniqueness moved me, and I'd trapped her in an absurdly American sexual script (overdose of unenlightened fucking, cheap hotel rooms, relentless physical intimacy, playacting). I can't say I began to tire of her, but it wasn't only the need to get back home, to catch my charter flight in London, that made me think of escape. (It had to be escape — I was incapable of telling her the truth, simply confessing to be nothing like what I'd pretended, not a "writer," not a bullfighter, someone with a life of his own, but just a college boy with a major in girls.) I may have regretted taking French leave of her, but I'd been so false and au fond I thought so little of myself, as a man or a mate, that I couldn't imagine my loss to her mattering very much.

A clear morning. I sneaked away, hitchhiked to Málaga, got on a train. I imagined her waking, waiting for me to return, growing disturbed, then I stopped imagining. Two hours later I was halfway to Madrid on the train. I can only say that there was a kind of ecstasy of freedom — a sick feeling of shame and relief. Because in the midst of all my falseness, all my hateful foolery and nonsense, there had been a fairly straightforward response: and it was to find her delicious, romantic, soulfully sublime, but for that very reason, not really for me.

Three days later Paris. I had to wait for F to show at our old hotel. I met a girl from Montreal, green eyes and pale skin, inky hair cut à la Piaf. Her Quebecois accent so irritated the waiter in the hotel restaurant that he required me to order for us both, using my high school French. I felt quite the man of parts, and she took me to some amusing haunts of hers, in the 16th arrondissement as I recall . . .

October 1992

Saturday, 11:00 o'clock

DEAR FATHER,

You must be a little surprised to hear from me after these years. Maybe you thought I had forgotten you, or I disappeared from the earth. I assure you, I still exist here, and I even begin to put together my life now, I think.

I have received three letters from you, including the very long one from our trip together. Don't think I never read them. Many times I wanted to respond to them. I waited till now because, as you see, I have found a copy of *Tango Mortale* for you. It's a very rare copy, because my mother destroyed all the copies she could find, a long time before she died.

Let me tell you about myself, it's simple. I live in Brussels now. I drive a taxicab. I take maths courses at the free university. I have very few friends. I don't have any women with me.

Sometimes, a big grief takes a long time to come home, like when you go to sleep one night and dream of running, and you wake in the morning to find you have no legs anymore. When I was happy to get to know you, looking forward to that, and thought that I had lost one parent, but I still had another, I was in that dream. I didn't know you, but I wanted to start from that point. I had just buried my mother, you know. I thought that it was over, it was very sad, but it was over.

Once you said to me, "No matter what they think about us, we are their Fate. We are the Fate that women have." I thought you sounded very clever when you said that. You didn't say that women are the Fate that men have, too, but maybe you meant that. I don't know.

You must have been my mother's Fate, then. I see that you were her Fate. And I feel so sad for her because of that. Because you didn't want to be her Fate. You just wanted to have her, enjoy her, make love, and it was a long time ago, maybe 25 years. It's not such a big crime, anyway. When I was living in Gent, I was already doing this with several girls. I think because I wanted to be like you.

We are their Fate, I think; but we have to let them be ours, too. I don't think you would ever let a woman be that for you, and that makes you strong, it makes you seem strong. A lot of women like that. It attracts them. This is another way that I wanted to be like you.

It makes a difference, though, what they think of us, the idea they have of us. My mother, let us say, had you for her

Fate, but then she refused to get over it, her whole life. She spent twenty-five years studying it. Without ever becoming crazy about it, always trying to live a decent life, being my wonderful mother to me always, she kept thinking about it, wondering about it. She wrote books of poetry about it. *Tango Mortale* is just the first one she wrote, when she felt you still like a Spanish knife in her heart. She wanted to twist away from you, and she only tore her heart when she did.

Later, she became quieter about it. She found it even funny. That something very casual had happened, a pretty woman meets a young man, they go on a trip together, they make love, and she has a baby. But something from it remained in her heart. She thought this was funny, that life would do this to her. Trick her somehow.

I wonder what you think about all this, and I feel angry at you now. You know — I really blame you. I owe you my life, there is a fact of biology, but you hurt my mother badly, and in some way I think she died because of that, because of you. You were pretending to have a heart to give to her, to hand forward in romance, but she really did have a heart like that. She lived for a while and then she wanted to die. She waited till I was grown up, I think. Life was a beautiful disappointment to her. It puzzled her.

I feel sad about her, and I think I have to live for a while feeling this way, with sadness. Right now, I don't want to be with any woman. When I can let a woman be my Fate, when I meet such a woman, if I ever do, maybe I can be with her then, I don't know. I'm not interested in many women, numbers of them, that seems a bad, hurting idea. I'm not like your son that way — I'm different. I don't admire your life of many adventures, lots of women, it isn't for me. It already seems like an old idea, something from the past — it's good people don't want that anymore.

I apologize, it isn't good that I don't write you for a long time. But please, don't think that I forget you. I never did have a father, you know, but then you were kind to meet me, you came to me and tried to be a little like a father. Maybe it was too late for us, but someday, I want to see you again. I know I have a sister in America, your daughter, who I only saw in a few pictures. I want to meet her someday. Tell her that she has a brother, too, and that he wants to know her. Someday we will sit down together, look each other in the eye, and know each other very well. Something good will start from that.

Your son,
Jean-Marc
17 Rue des Étrangères
Brussels 1170